MAX STEEL™

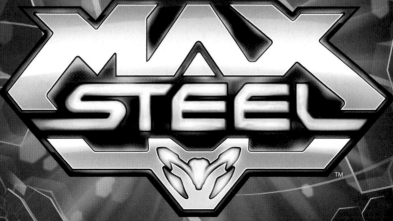

VOLUME 1
•THE PARASITES•

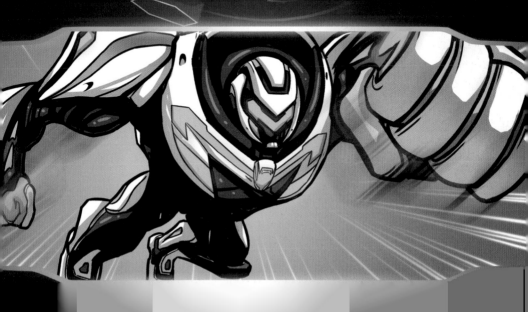

max steel™
Volume 1
The Parasites

Story by Brian Smith
Art by Jan Wijngaard
Letters by Infinitoons

Design/Sam Elzway
Editor/Joel Enos

Special thanks to Gabriel DeLaTorre, Lloyd Goldfine, Cindy Ledermann, Michael Montalvo, Jocelyn Morgan, Julia Phelps and Darren Sander.

Printed in the U.S.A.

Published by VIZ Media, LLC
P.O. Box 77010
San Francisco, CA 94107

10 9 8 7 6 5 4 3 2 1
First printing, September 2013

VOLUME 1
•THE PARASITES•

TABLE OF CONTENTS

WHAT IF THE ULTIMATE SUPERPOWER CAME WITH A MIND OF ITS OWN?

To the world at large, turbocharged Max Steel is the newest, coolest, most beloved superhero. To the secret organization of N-Tek, he's their number one ally in the ongoing fight against mayhem, monsters and alien invasion. And to supervillains, he's the only source of Turbo Energy in the universe and therefore incredibly valuable and sought after—by

MAX & STEEL

Two heads are better than one, unless one belongs to a stubborn teenager and the other belongs to a headstrong alien. Somehow, these two have to learn to cooperate as one entity, superhero Max Steel, protector of the universe!

KIRBY

Max's best friend at school is always on the lookout for fun, adventure and hijinks.

SYDNEY

The girl Max likes is also one of his best friends. But super-heroics often ruin any attempt to take this friendship to the next level.

MOLLY

Max's mom is an ex-agent of N-Tek, the secret group that Max relies on for his high-tech support and guidance.

any means necessary. But really, he's just 16-year-old Maxwell McGrath, former regular guy, who's got a whole bunch of crazy new powers and now has to figure out how to live constantly connected (and sometimes merged) to N'Baro AksSteel X377, a wisecracking alien with an attitude who's not always the most cooperative partner. Together, these two friends from different worlds combine to make one superhero...and will have to figure out how to save the universe!

N-TEK

A highly secret, super-scientific organization that protects Earth from technological and biological threats. Founded twenty years ago by Forge Ferrus (now the head of N-Tek), Miles Dredd and Jim McGrath (Max's father), N-Tek and its agents use advanced alien technology to aid Max in his role as Earth's best hope from invasion.

BERTO

KAT

FORGE

DREDD

The former co-founder of N-Tek went rogue after a heated argument resulted in an explosion and the disappearance of Max's father, Jim McGrath. Now fused with a Turbo Energy siphon into his own body, which he needs to fuse with Turbo Energy to stay alive, Dredd is constantly on the hunt for more Turbo—which is why he's after Max.

NAUGHT

Dredd's right-hand henchman has some diabolical designs of his own. He may seem like a nerd but he's still a formidable foe.

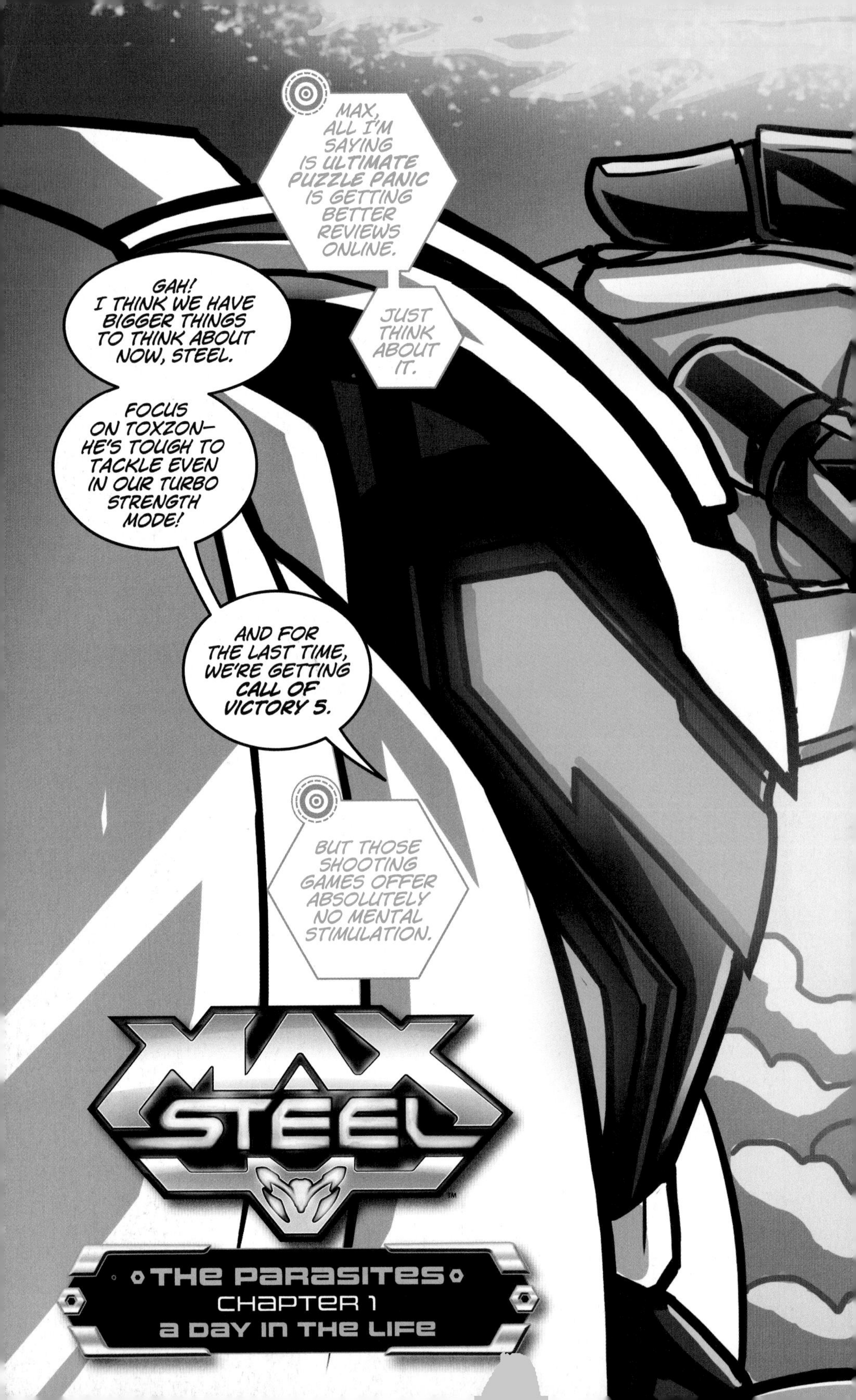
MAX, ALL I'M SAYING IS ULTIMATE PUZZLE PANIC IS GETTING BETTER REVIEWS ONLINE.
JUST THINK ABOUT IT.
GAH! I THINK WE HAVE BIGGER THINGS TO THINK ABOUT NOW, STEEL.
FOCUS ON TOXZON—HE'S TOUGH TO TACKLE EVEN IN OUR TURBO STRENGTH MODE!
AND FOR THE LAST TIME, WE'RE GETTING CALL OF VICTORY 5.
BUT THOSE SHOOTING GAMES OFFER ABSOLUTELY NO MENTAL STIMULATION.
MAX STEEL™
THE PARASITES
CHAPTER 1
A DAY IN THE LIFE

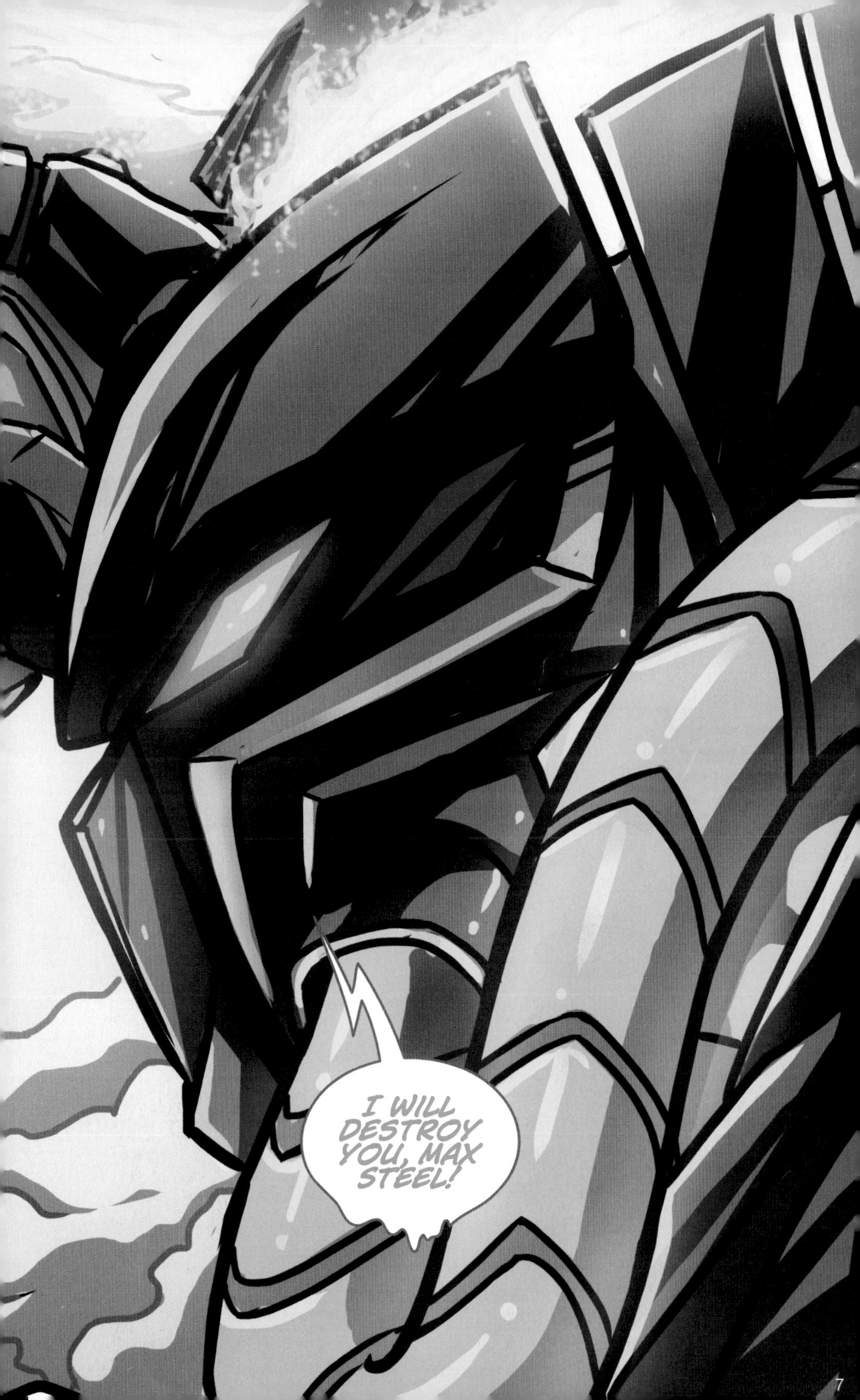
I WILL DESTROY YOU, MAX STEEL!

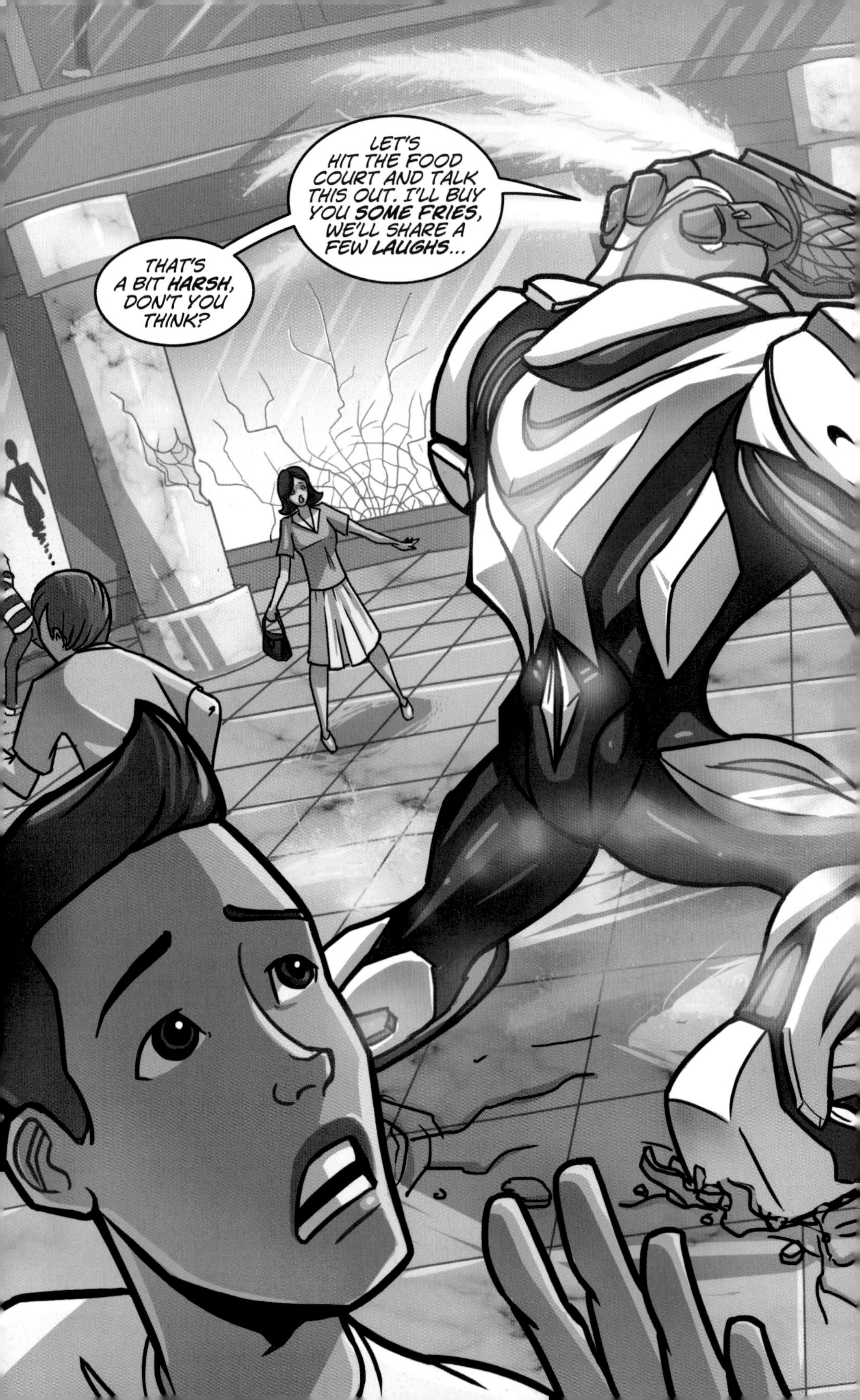
THAT'S A BIT HARSH, DON'T YOU THINK?
LET'S HIT THE FOOD COURT AND TALK THIS OUT. I'LL BUY YOU SOME FRIES, WE'LL SHARE A FEW LAUGHS...

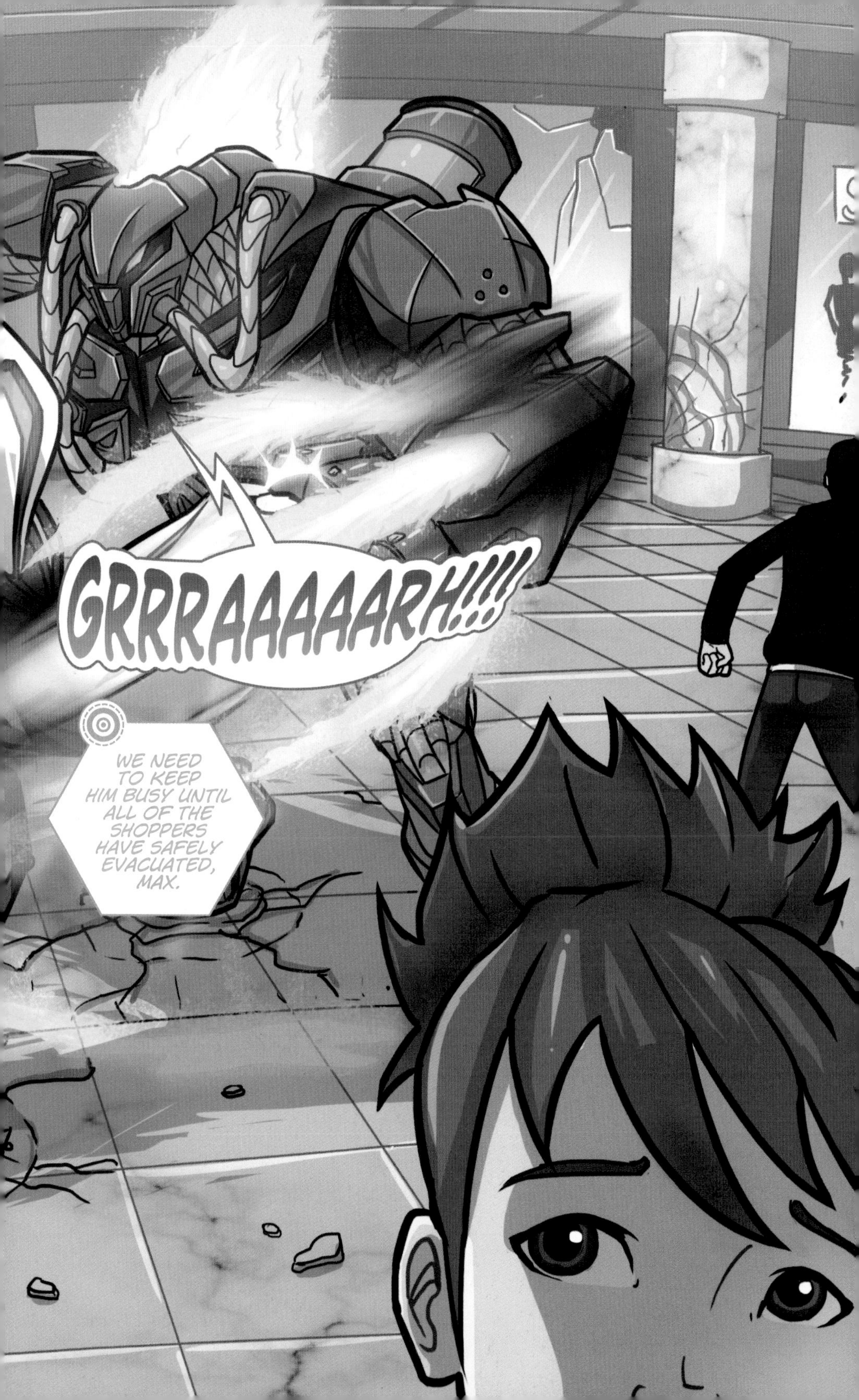
GRRRAAAAAARH!!!
WE NEED TO KEEP HIM BUSY UNTIL ALL OF THE SHOPPERS HAVE SAFELY EVACUATED, MAX.

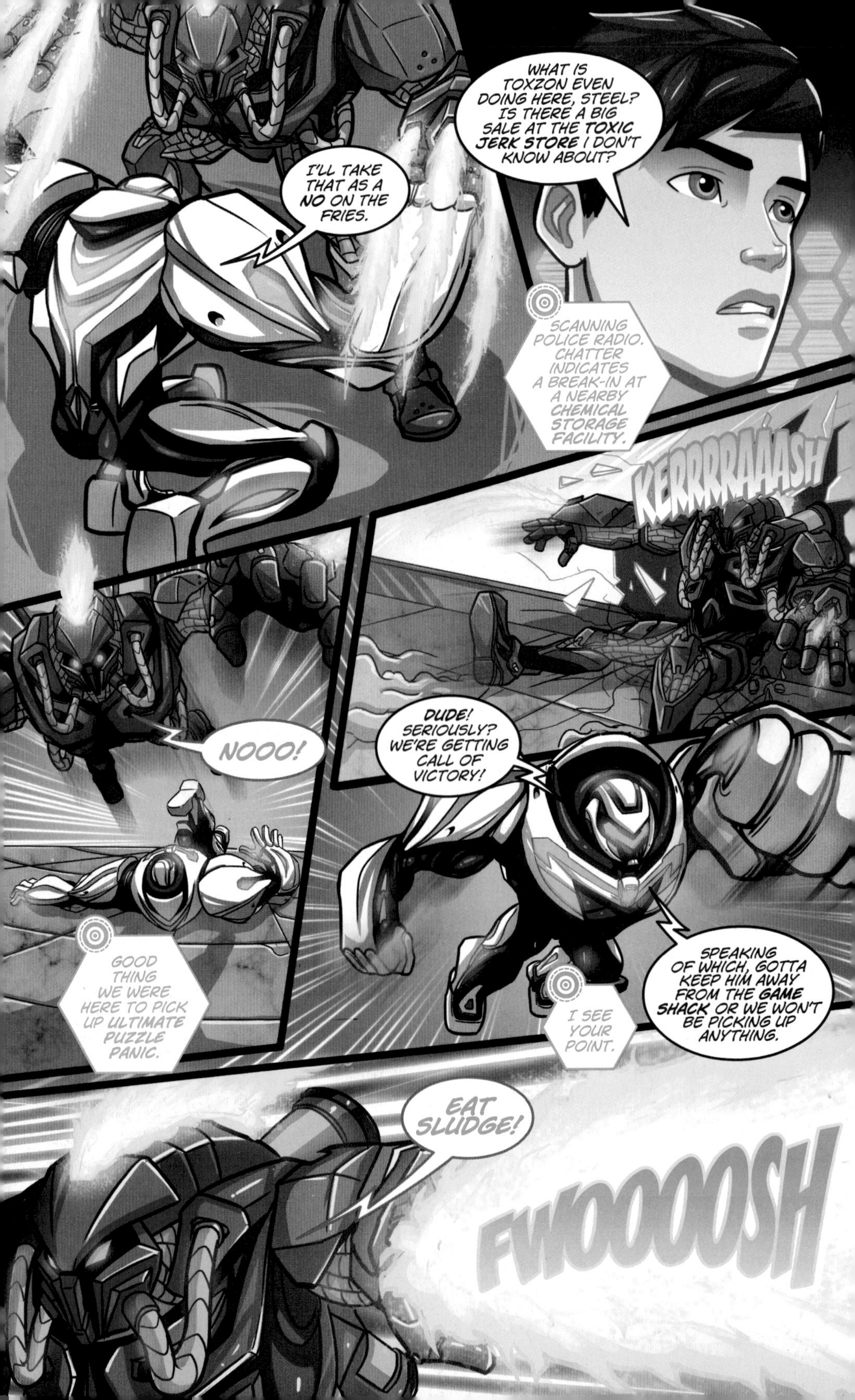
WHAT IS TOXZON EVEN DOING HERE, STEEL? IS THERE A BIG SALE AT THE TOXIC JERK STORE I DON'T KNOW ABOUT?
I'LL TAKE THAT AS A NO ON THE FRIES.
SCANNING POLICE RADIO. CHATTER INDICATES A BREAK-IN AT A NEARBY CHEMICAL STORAGE FACILITY.
KERRRRAAASH
NOOO!
GOOD THING WE WERE HERE TO PICK UP ULTIMATE PUZZLE PANIC.
DUDE! SERIOUSLY? WE'RE GETTING CALL OF VICTORY!
SPEAKING OF WHICH, GOTTA KEEP HIM AWAY FROM THE GAME SHACK OR WE WON'T BE PICKING UP ANYTHING.
I SEE YOUR POINT.
EAT SLUDGE!
FWOOOOOSH

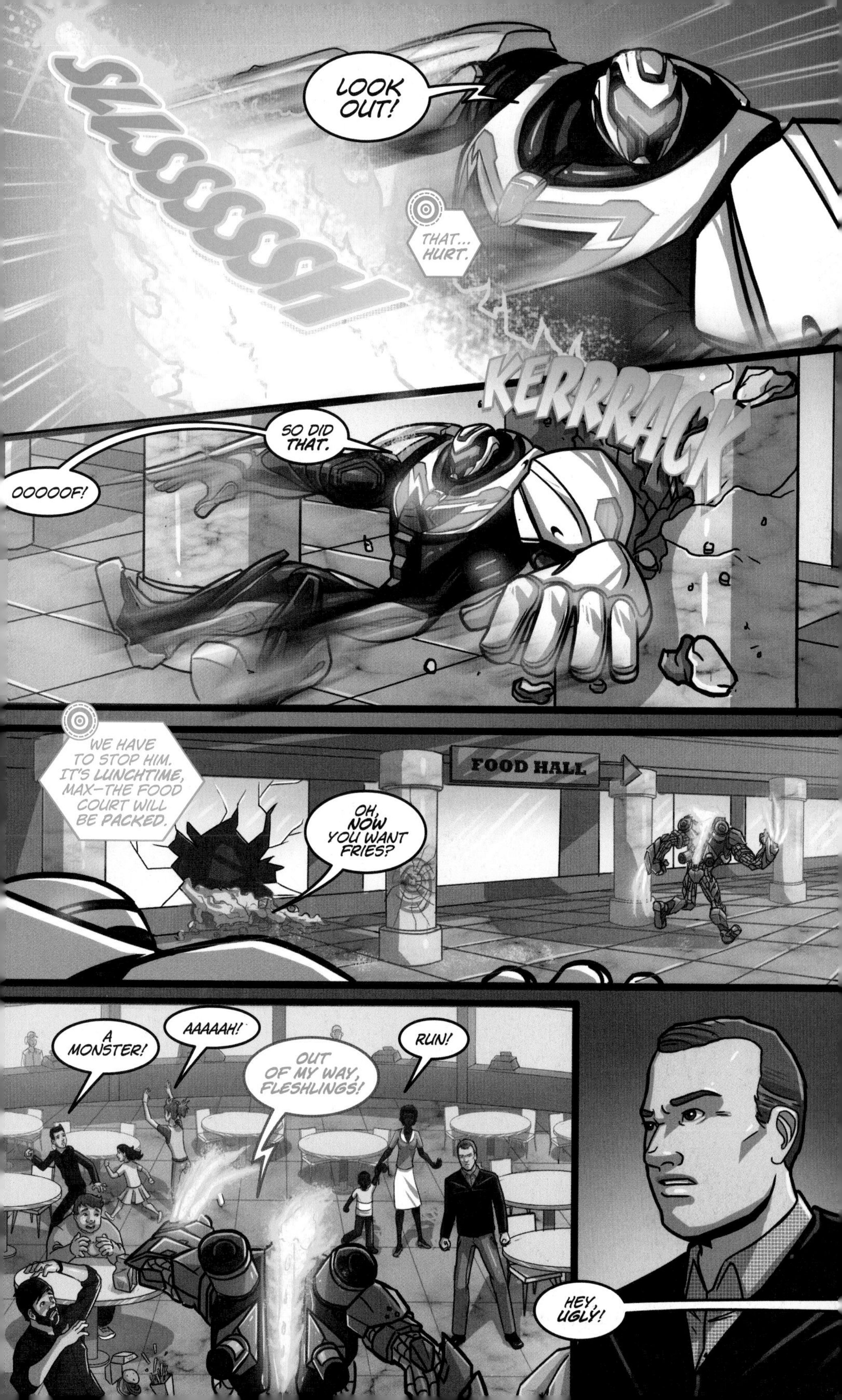
SSSSSSSH
LOOK OUT!
THAT... HURT.
KERRRACK
SO DID THAT.
OOOOOF!
WE HAVE TO STOP HIM. IT'S LUNCHTIME, MAX—THE FOOD COURT WILL BE PACKED.
FOOD HALL
OH, NOW YOU WANT FRIES?
A MONSTER!
AAAAAH!
OUT OF MY WAY, FLESHLINGS!
RUN!
HEY, UGLY!

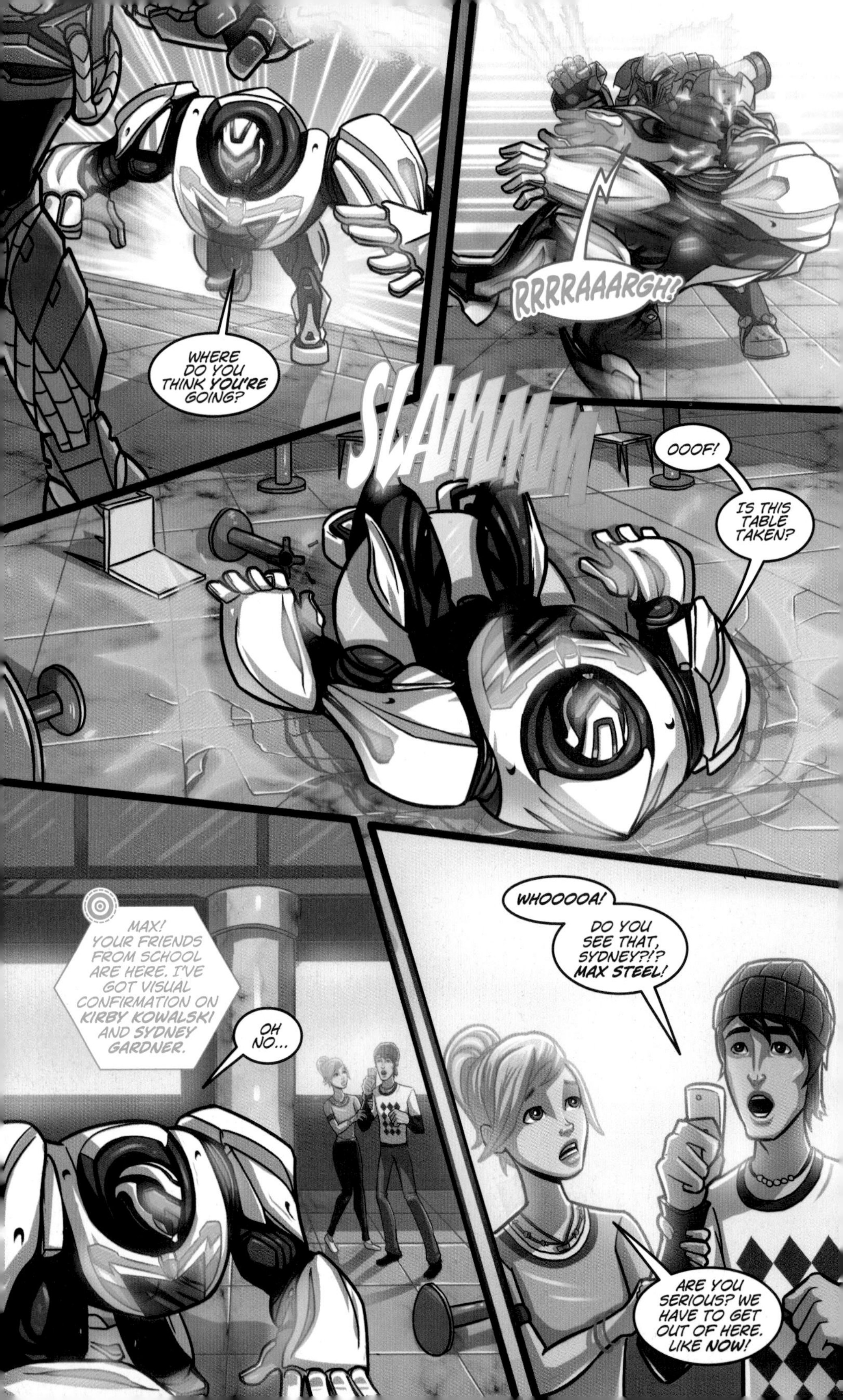
WHERE DO YOU THINK YOU'RE GOING?
RRRRAAARGH!
SLAMMMM
OOOF!
IS THIS TABLE TAKEN?
MAX! YOUR FRIENDS FROM SCHOOL ARE HERE. I'VE GOT VISUAL CONFIRMATION ON KIRBY KOWALSKI AND SYDNEY GARDNER.
OH NO...
WHOOOOA!
DO YOU SEE THAT, SYDNEY?!? MAX STEEL!
ARE YOU SERIOUS? WE HAVE TO GET OUT OF HERE. LIKE NOW!

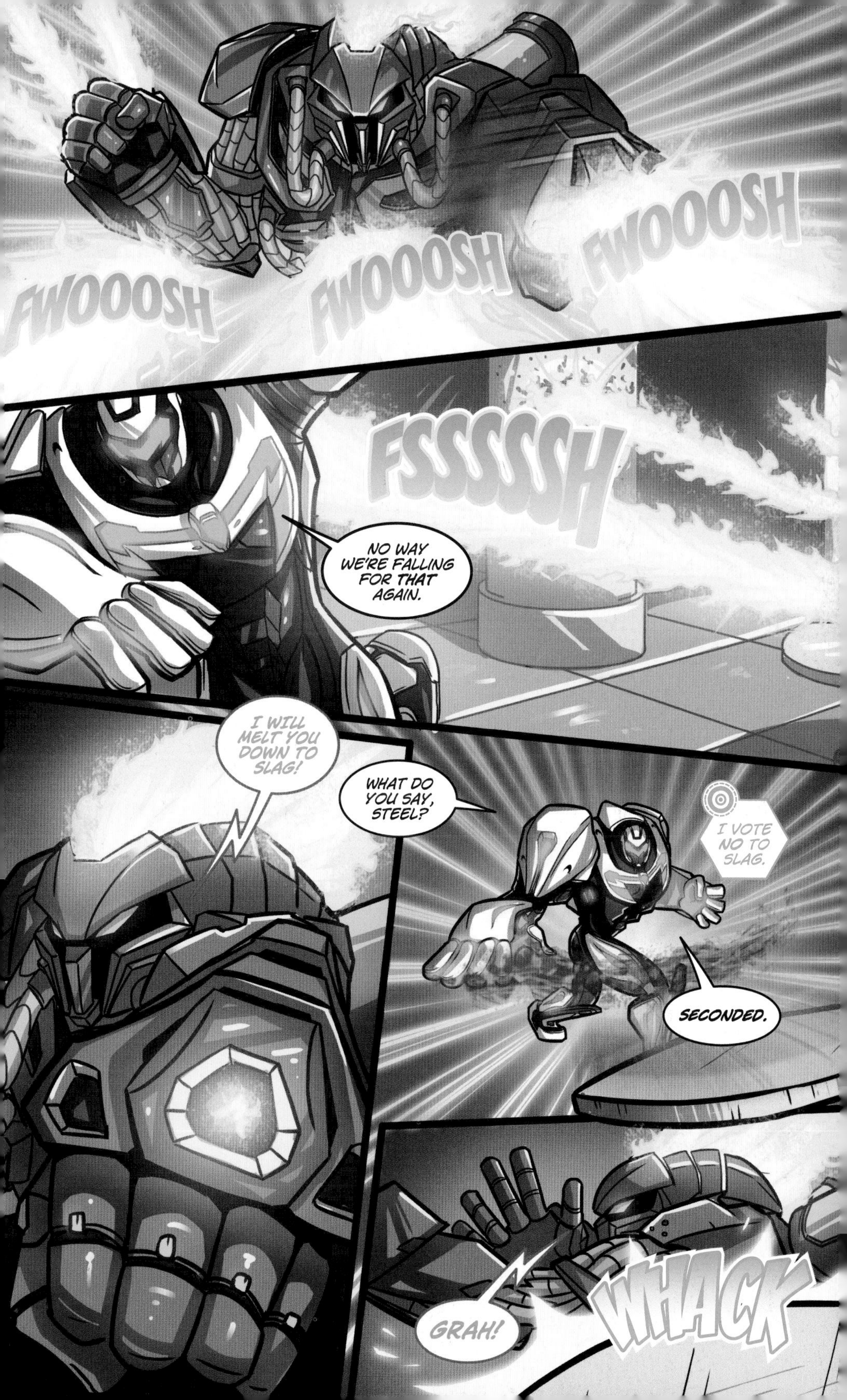
FWOOOSH
FWOOOSH
FWOOOSH
FSSSSSH
NO WAY WE'RE FALLING FOR THAT AGAIN.
I WILL MELT YOU DOWN TO SLAG!
WHAT DO YOU SAY, STEEL?
I VOTE NO TO SLAG.
SECONDED.
GRAH!
WHACK

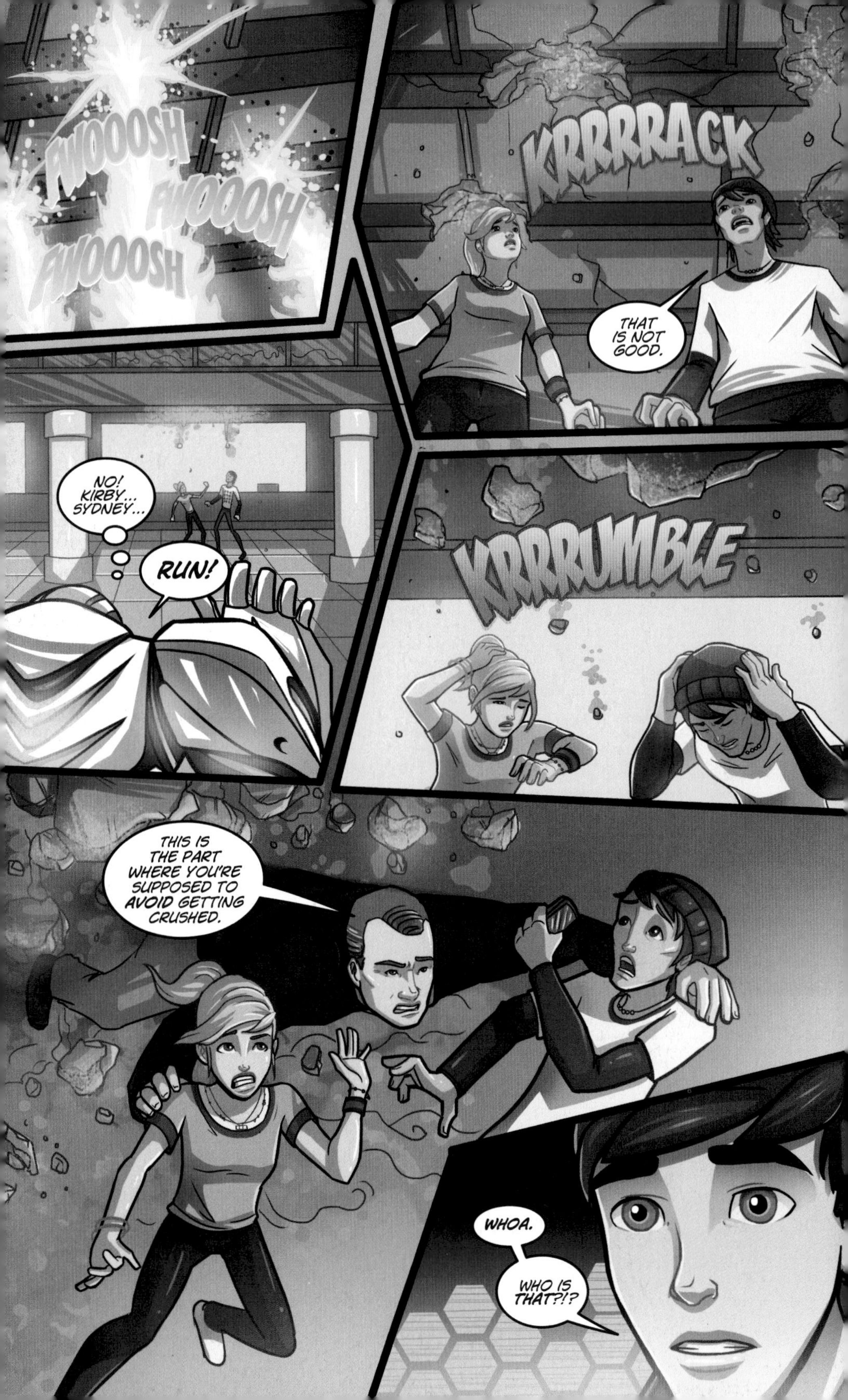
FWOOOSH
FWOOOSH
FWOOOSH
KRRRRACK
THAT IS NOT GOOD.
NO! KIRBY... SYDNEY...
RUN!
KRRRUMBLE
THIS IS THE PART WHERE YOU'RE SUPPOSED TO AVOID GETTING CRUSHED.
WHOA.
WHO IS THAT?!?

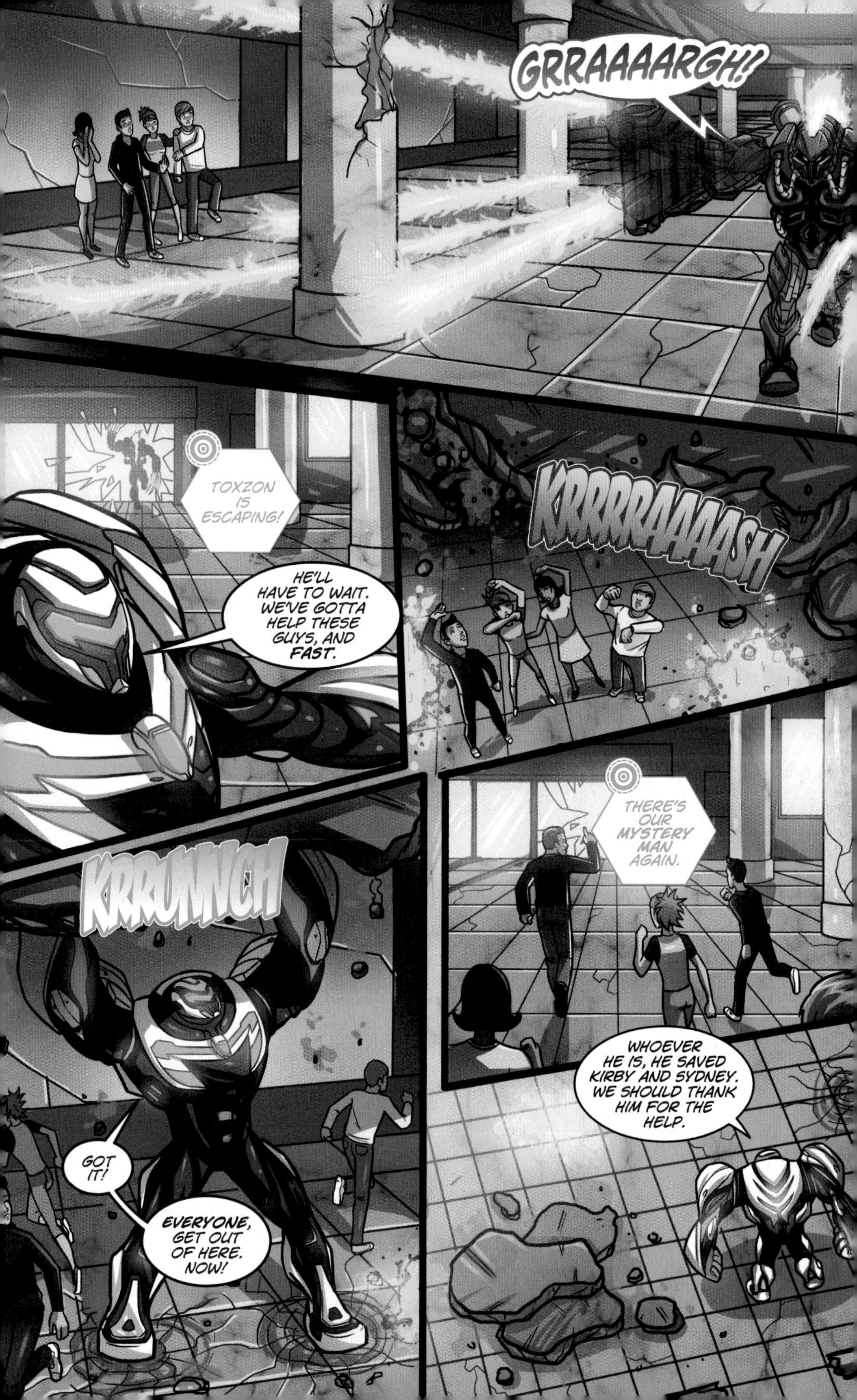
GRRAAAARGH!
TOXZON IS ESCAPING!
HE'LL HAVE TO WAIT. WE'VE GOTTA HELP THESE GUYS, AND FAST.
KRRRRAAAAASH
KRRUNNCH
GOT IT!
EVERYONE, GET OUT OF HERE. NOW!
THERE'S OUR MYSTERY MAN AGAIN.
WHOEVER HE IS, HE SAVED KIRBY AND SYDNEY. WE SHOULD THANK HIM FOR THE HELP.

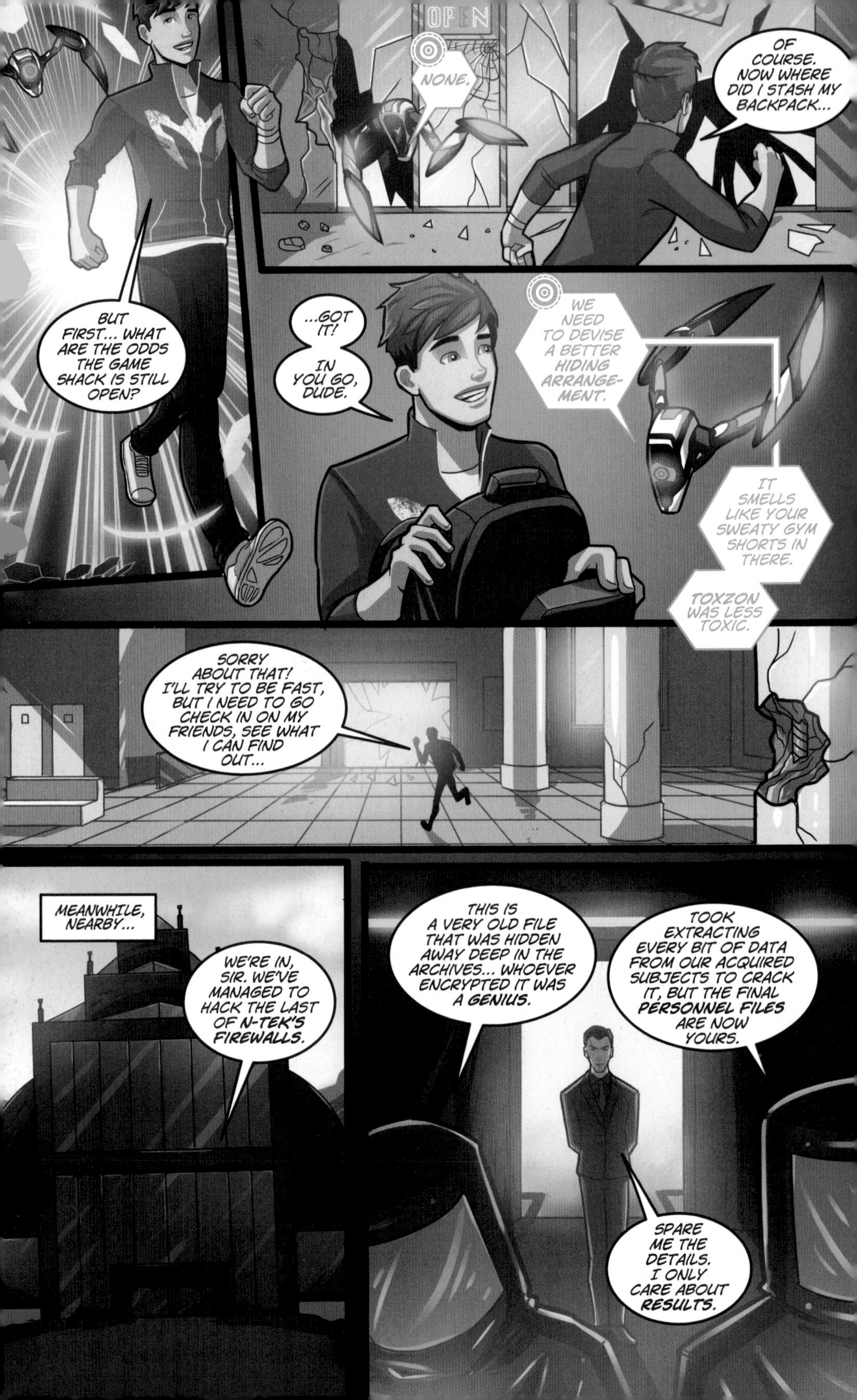
BUT FIRST... WHAT ARE THE ODDS THE GAME SHACK IS STILL OPEN?
OPEN
NONE.
OF COURSE. NOW WHERE DID I STASH MY BACKPACK...
...GOT IT!
IN YOU GO, DUDE.
WE NEED TO DEVISE A BETTER HIDING ARRANGE-MENT.
IT SMELLS LIKE YOUR SWEATY GYM SHORTS IN THERE.
TOXZON WAS LESS TOXIC.
SORRY ABOUT THAT! I'LL TRY TO BE FAST, BUT I NEED TO GO CHECK IN ON MY FRIENDS, SEE WHAT I CAN FIND OUT...
MEANWHILE, NEARBY...
WE'RE IN, SIR. WE'VE MANAGED TO HACK THE LAST OF N-TEK'S FIREWALLS.
THIS IS A VERY OLD FILE THAT WAS HIDDEN AWAY DEEP IN THE ARCHIVES... WHOEVER ENCRYPTED IT WAS A GENIUS.
TOOK EXTRACTING EVERY BIT OF DATA FROM OUR ACQUIRED SUBJECTS TO CRACK IT, BUT THE FINAL PERSONNEL FILES ARE NOW YOURS.
SPARE ME THE DETAILS. I ONLY CARE ABOUT RESULTS.

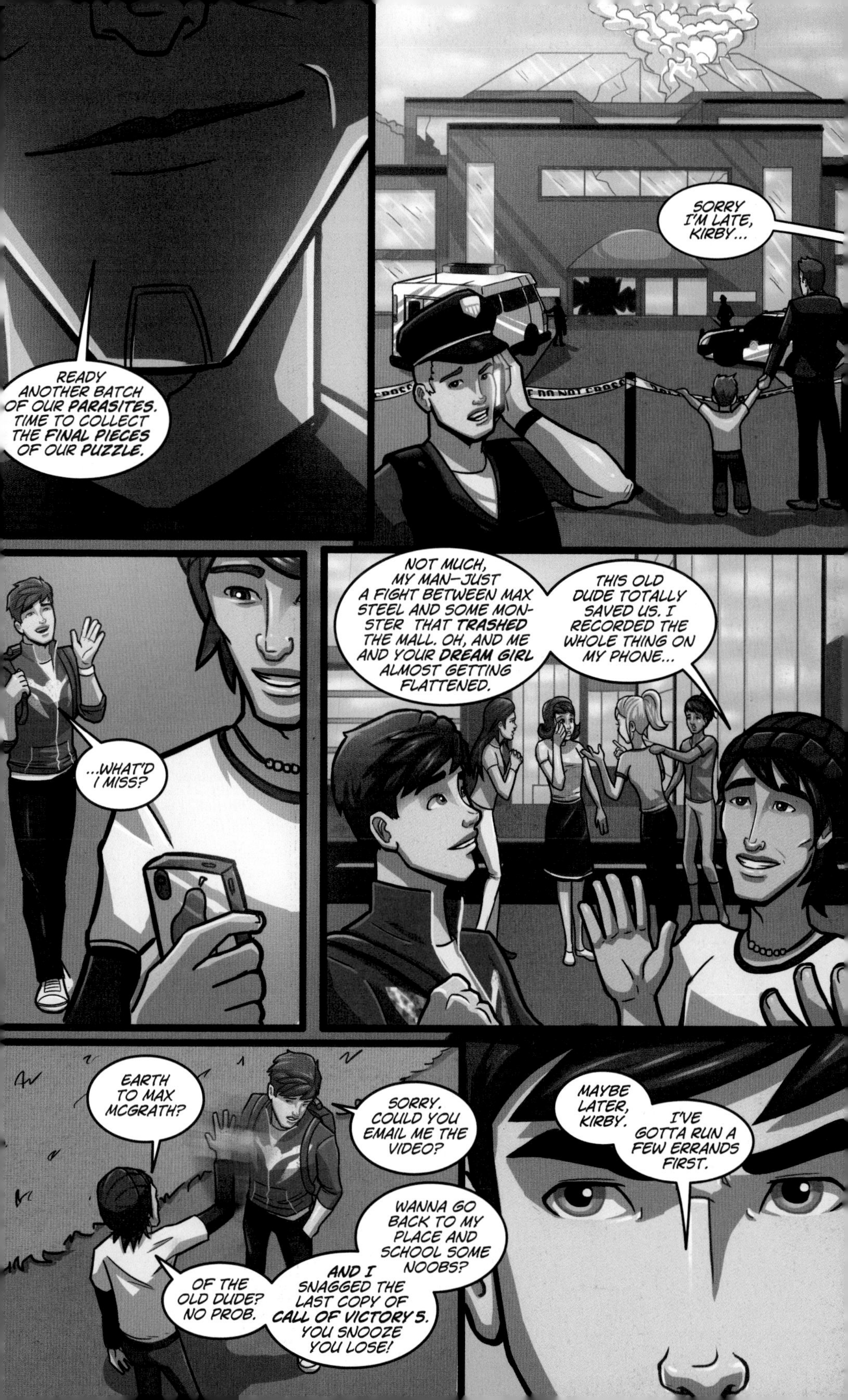
READY ANOTHER BATCH OF OUR PARASITES. TIME TO COLLECT THE FINAL PIECES OF OUR PUZZLE.
SORRY I'M LATE, KIRBY...
...WHAT'D I MISS?
NOT MUCH, MY MAN—JUST A FIGHT BETWEEN MAX STEEL AND SOME MONSTER THAT TRASHED THE MALL. OH, AND ME AND YOUR DREAM GIRL ALMOST GETTING FLATTENED.
THIS OLD DUDE TOTALLY SAVED US. I RECORDED THE WHOLE THING ON MY PHONE...
EARTH TO MAX MCGRATH?
SORRY. COULD YOU EMAIL ME THE VIDEO?
OF THE OLD DUDE? NO PROB.
WANNA GO BACK TO MY PLACE AND SCHOOL SOME NOOBS?
AND I SNAGGED THE LAST COPY OF CALL OF VICTORY 5. YOU SNOOZE YOU LOSE!
MAYBE LATER, KIRBY.
I'VE GOTTA RUN A FEW ERRANDS FIRST.

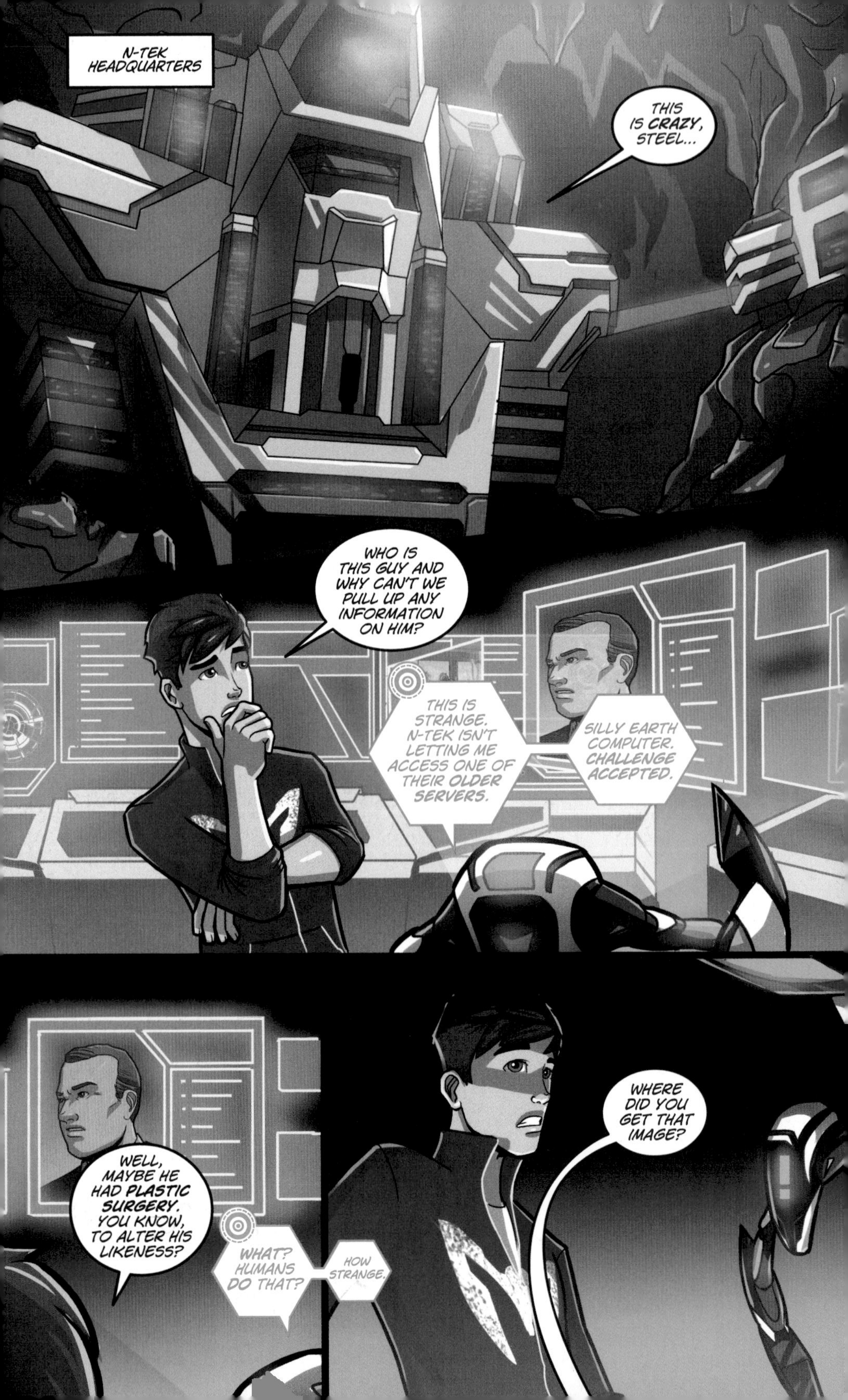
N-TEK HEADQUARTERS
THIS IS CRAZY, STEEL...
WHO IS THIS GUY AND WHY CAN'T WE PULL UP ANY INFORMATION ON HIM?
THIS IS STRANGE. N-TEK ISN'T LETTING ME ACCESS ONE OF THEIR OLDER SERVERS.
SILLY EARTH COMPUTER. CHALLENGE ACCEPTED.
WELL, MAYBE HE HAD PLASTIC SURGERY. YOU KNOW, TO ALTER HIS LIKENESS?
WHAT? HUMANS DO THAT?
HOW STRANGE.
WHERE DID YOU GET THAT IMAGE?

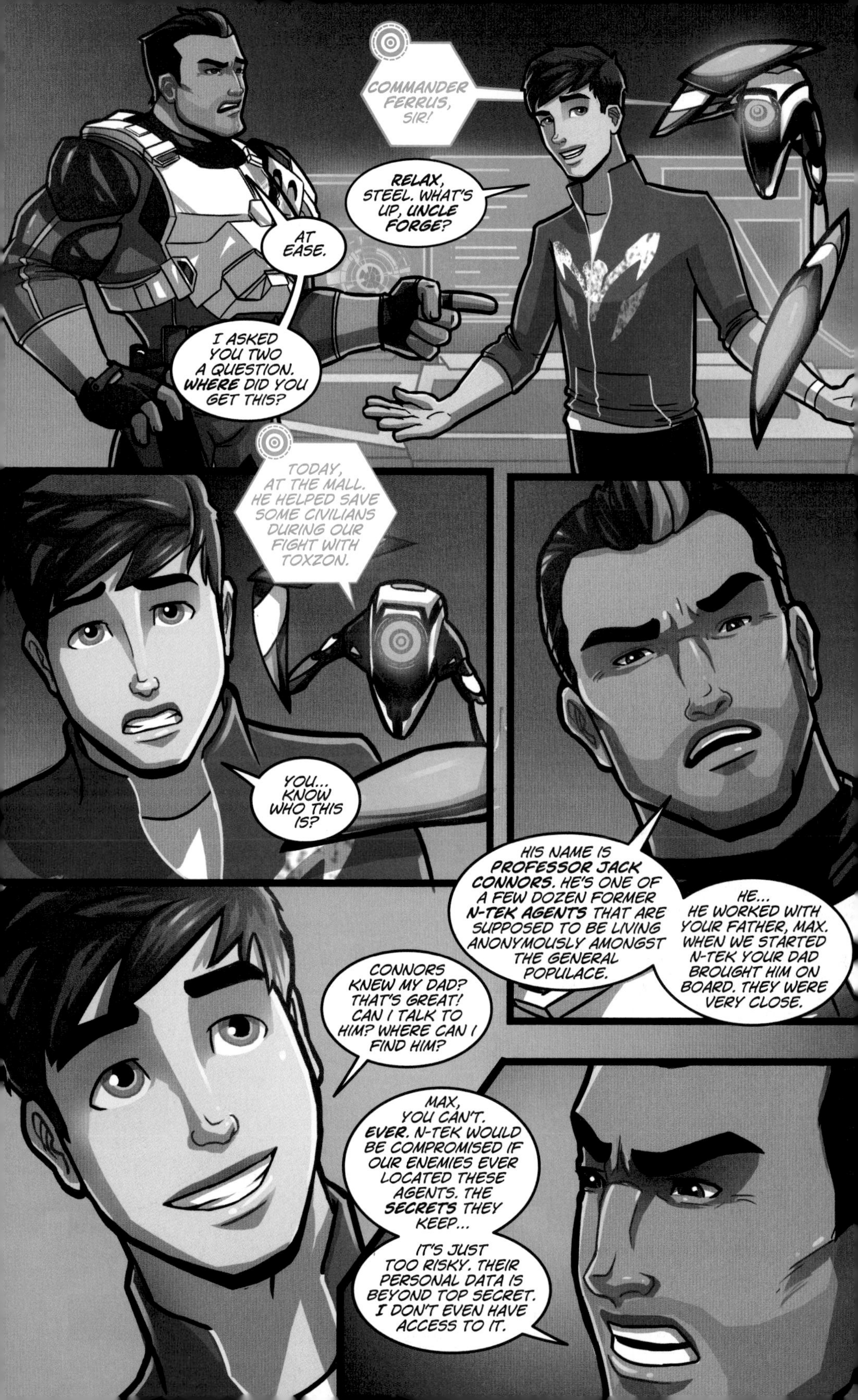
COMMANDER FERRUS, SIR!
AT EASE.
RELAX, STEEL. WHAT'S UP, UNCLE FORGE?
I ASKED YOU TWO A QUESTION. WHERE DID YOU GET THIS?
TODAY, AT THE MALL. HE HELPED SAVE SOME CIVILIANS DURING OUR FIGHT WITH TOXZON.
YOU... KNOW WHO THIS IS?
HIS NAME IS PROFESSOR JACK CONNORS. HE'S ONE OF A FEW DOZEN FORMER N-TEK AGENTS THAT ARE SUPPOSED TO BE LIVING ANONYMOUSLY AMONGST THE GENERAL POPULACE.
HE... HE WORKED WITH YOUR FATHER, MAX. WHEN WE STARTED N-TEK YOUR DAD BROUGHT HIM ON BOARD. THEY WERE VERY CLOSE.
CONNORS KNEW MY DAD? THAT'S GREAT! CAN I TALK TO HIM? WHERE CAN I FIND HIM?
MAX, YOU CAN'T. EVER. N-TEK WOULD BE COMPROMISED IF OUR ENEMIES EVER LOCATED THESE AGENTS. THE SECRETS THEY KEEP...
IT'S JUST TOO RISKY. THEIR PERSONAL DATA IS BEYOND TOP SECRET. I DON'T EVEN HAVE ACCESS TO IT.

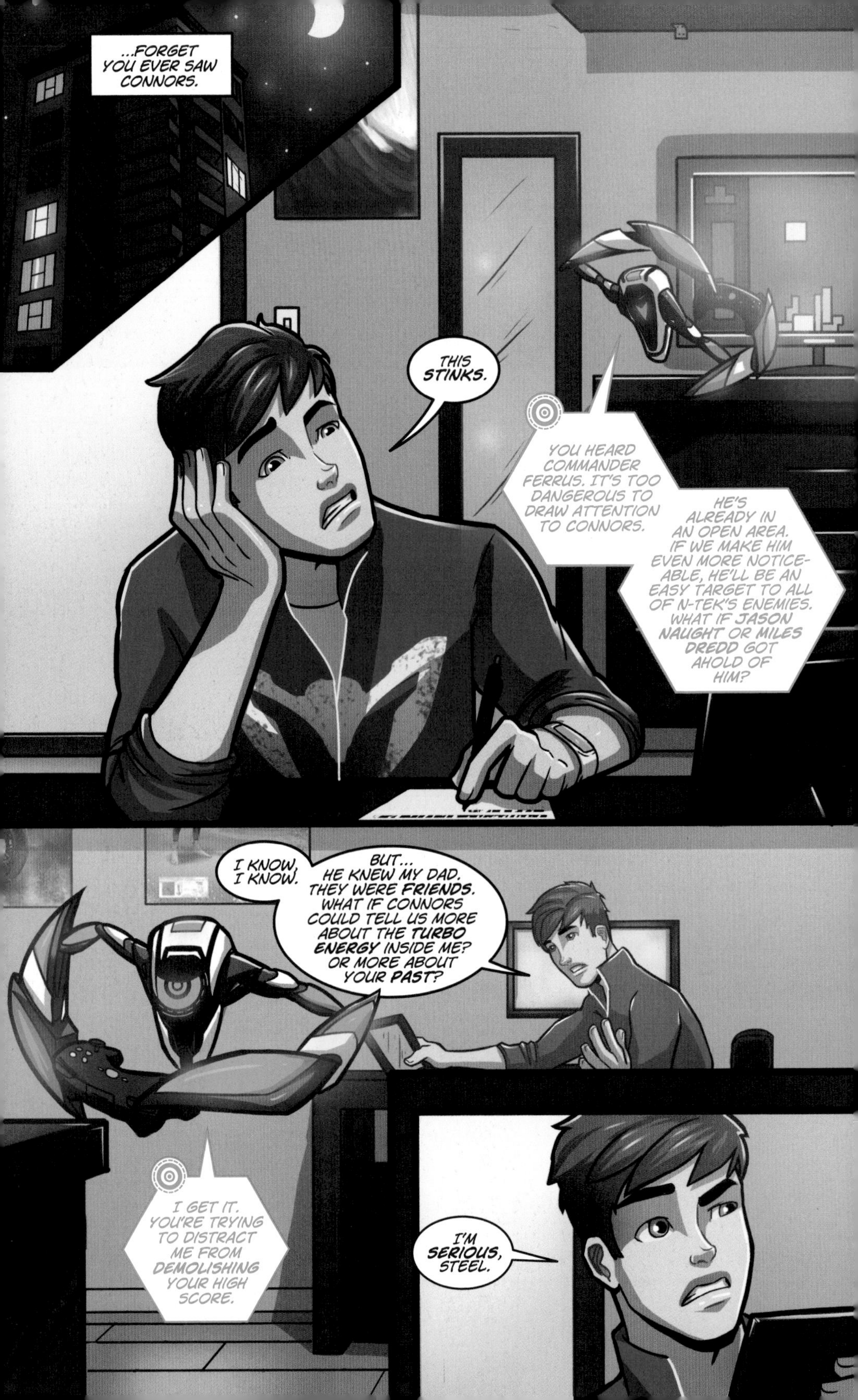
...FORGET YOU EVER SAW CONNORS.
THIS STINKS.
YOU HEARD COMMANDER FERRUS. IT'S TOO DANGEROUS TO DRAW ATTENTION TO CONNORS.
HE'S ALREADY IN AN OPEN AREA. IF WE MAKE HIM EVEN MORE NOTICE-ABLE, HE'LL BE AN EASY TARGET TO ALL OF N-TEK'S ENEMIES. WHAT IF JASON NAUGHT OR MILES DREDD GOT AHOLD OF HIM?
I KNOW, I KNOW.
BUT... HE KNEW MY DAD. THEY WERE FRIENDS. WHAT IF CONNORS COULD TELL US MORE ABOUT THE TURBO ENERGY INSIDE ME? OR MORE ABOUT YOUR PAST?
I GET IT. YOU'RE TRYING TO DISTRACT ME FROM DEMOLISHING YOUR HIGH SCORE.
I'M SERIOUS, STEEL.

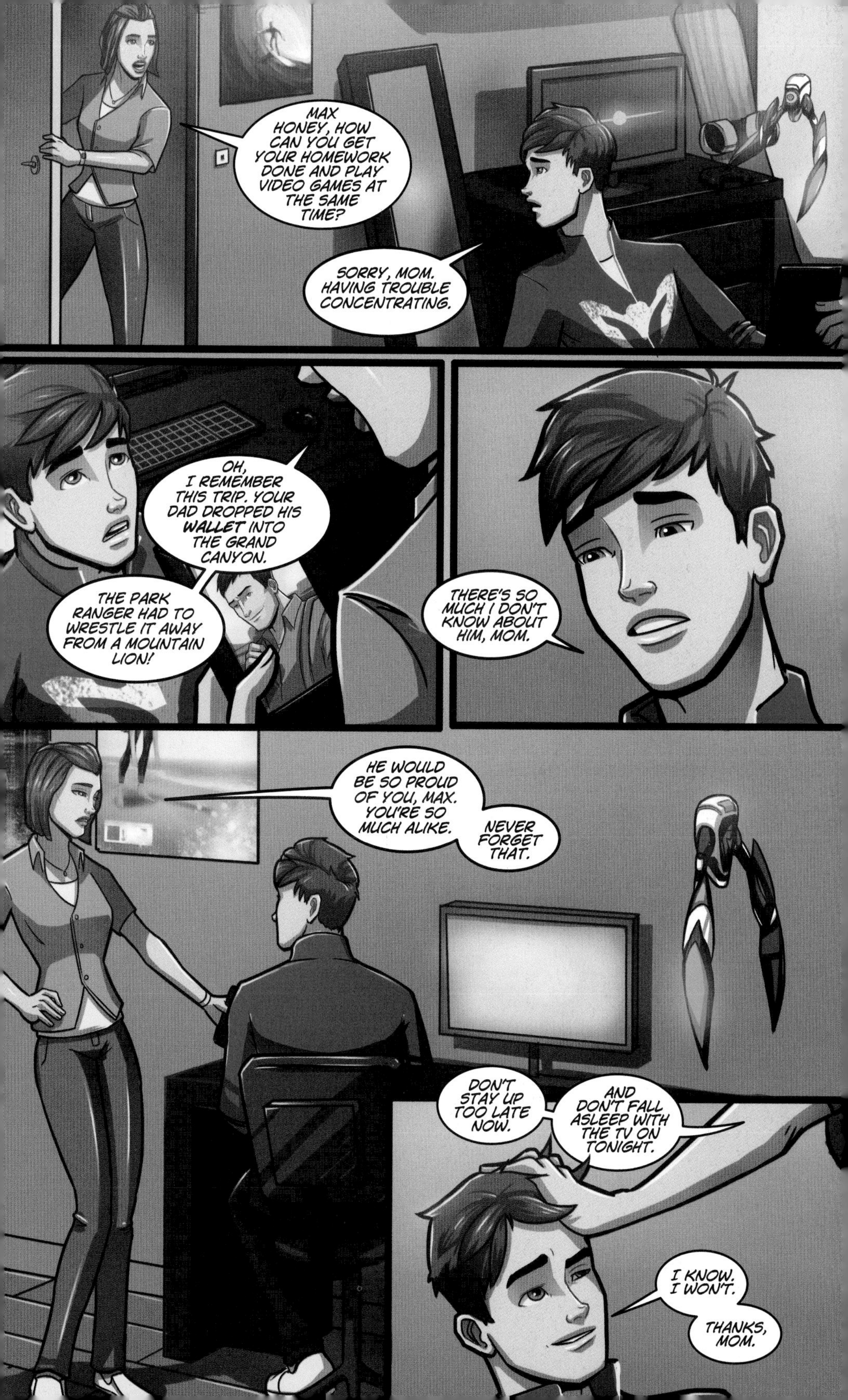
MAX HONEY, HOW CAN YOU GET YOUR HOMEWORK DONE AND PLAY VIDEO GAMES AT THE SAME TIME?
SORRY, MOM. HAVING TROUBLE CONCENTRATING.
OH, I REMEMBER THIS TRIP. YOUR DAD DROPPED HIS WALLET INTO THE GRAND CANYON.
THE PARK RANGER HAD TO WRESTLE IT AWAY FROM A MOUNTAIN LION!
THERE'S SO MUCH I DON'T KNOW ABOUT HIM, MOM.
HE WOULD BE SO PROUD OF YOU, MAX. YOU'RE SO MUCH ALIKE.
NEVER FORGET THAT.
DON'T STAY UP TOO LATE NOW.
AND DON'T FALL ASLEEP WITH THE TV ON TONIGHT.
I KNOW. I WON'T.
THANKS, MOM.

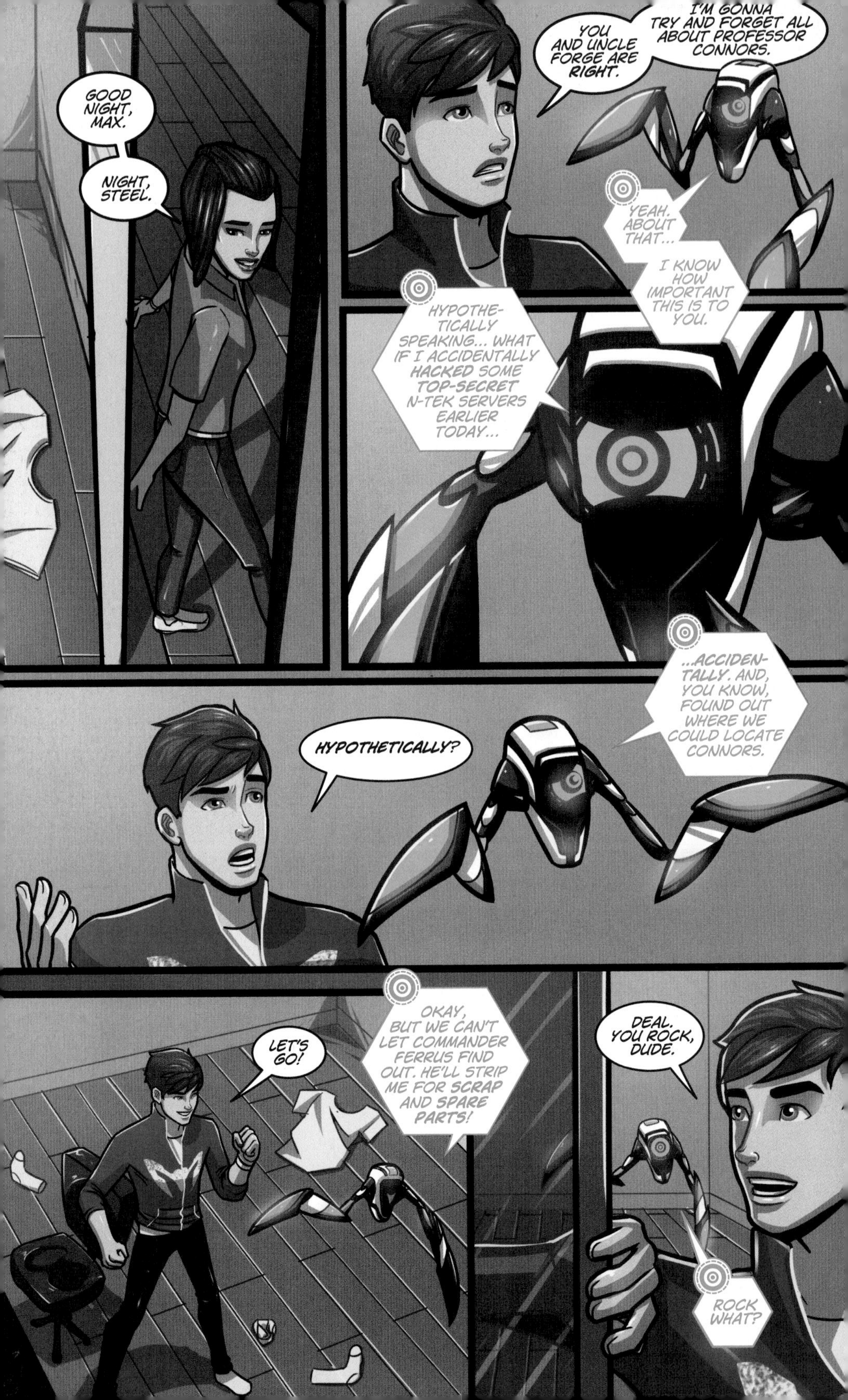
GOOD NIGHT, MAX.
NIGHT, STEEL.
YOU AND UNCLE FORGE ARE RIGHT.
I'M GONNA TRY AND FORGET ALL ABOUT PROFESSOR CONNORS.
YEAH. ABOUT THAT...
I KNOW HOW IMPORTANT THIS IS TO YOU.
HYPOTHETICALLY SPEAKING... WHAT IF I ACCIDENTALLY HACKED SOME TOP-SECRET N-TEK SERVERS EARLIER TODAY...
HYPOTHETICALLY?
...ACCIDENTALLY. AND, YOU KNOW, FOUND OUT WHERE WE COULD LOCATE CONNORS.
LET'S GO!
OKAY, BUT WE CAN'T LET COMMANDER FERRUS FIND OUT. HE'LL STRIP ME FOR SCRAP AND SPARE PARTS!
DEAL. YOU ROCK, DUDE.
ROCK WHAT?

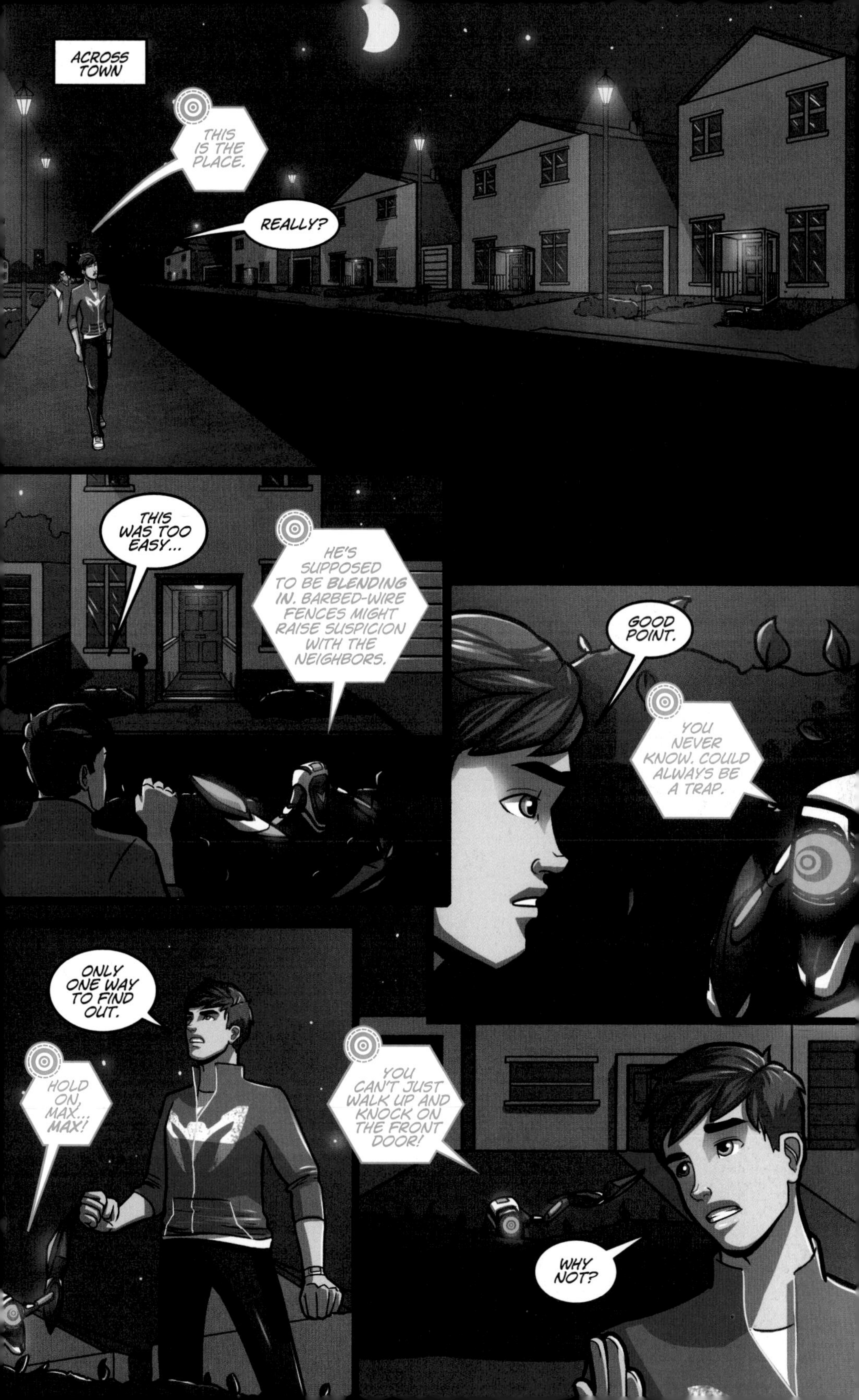
ACROSS TOWN
THIS IS THE PLACE.
REALLY?
THIS WAS TOO EASY...
HE'S SUPPOSED TO BE BLENDING IN. BARBED-WIRE FENCES MIGHT RAISE SUSPICION WITH THE NEIGHBORS.
GOOD POINT.
YOU NEVER KNOW. COULD ALWAYS BE A TRAP.
ONLY ONE WAY TO FIND OUT.
HOLD ON, MAX... MAX!
YOU CAN'T JUST WALK UP AND KNOCK ON THE FRONT DOOR!
WHY NOT?

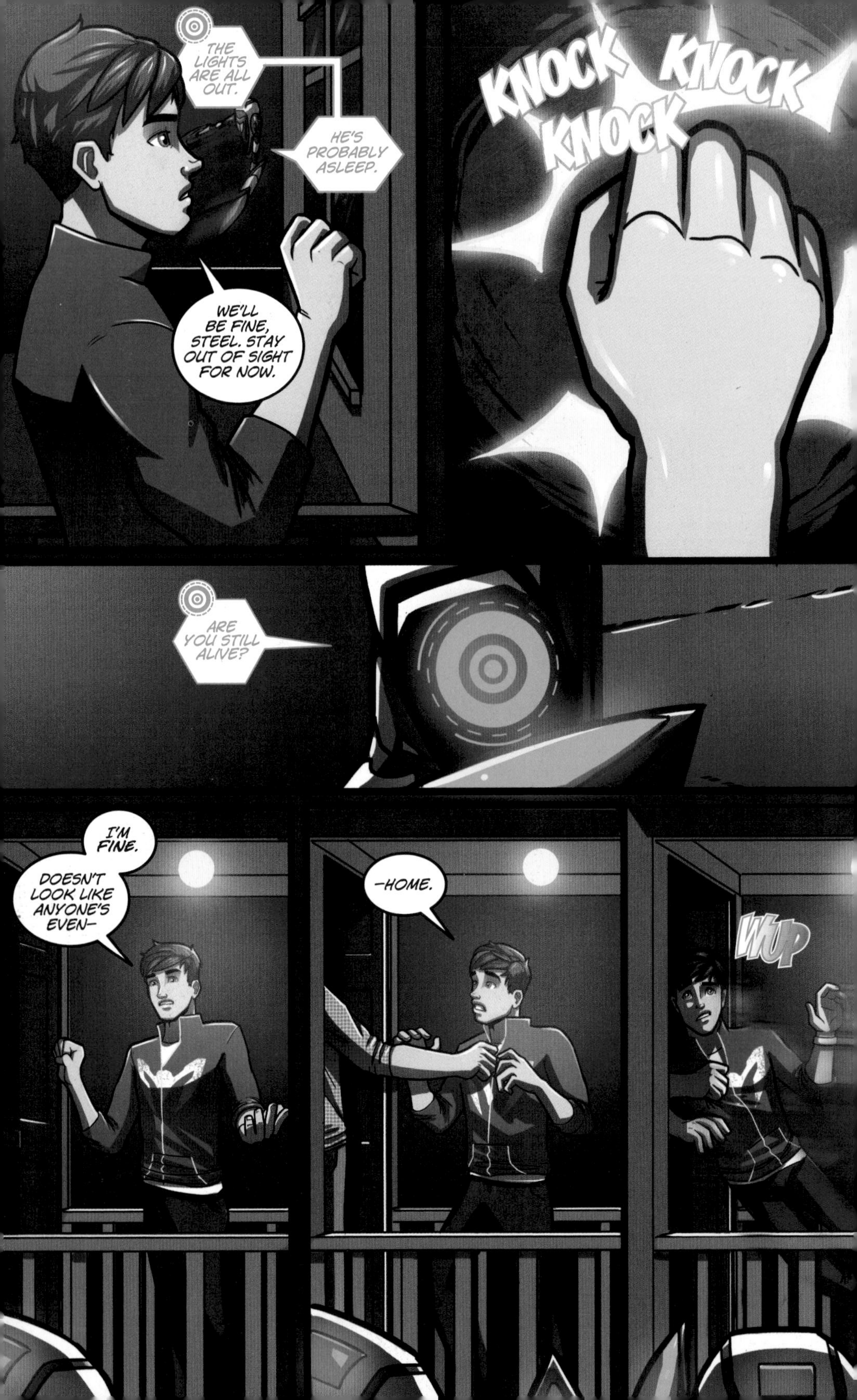
THE LIGHTS ARE ALL OUT.
HE'S PROBABLY ASLEEP.
WE'LL BE FINE, STEEL. STAY OUT OF SIGHT FOR NOW.
KNOCK KNOCK KNOCK
ARE YOU STILL ALIVE?
I'M FINE.
DOESN'T LOOK LIKE ANYONE'S EVEN-
-HOME.
WUP

CHAPTER 2: CONNORS

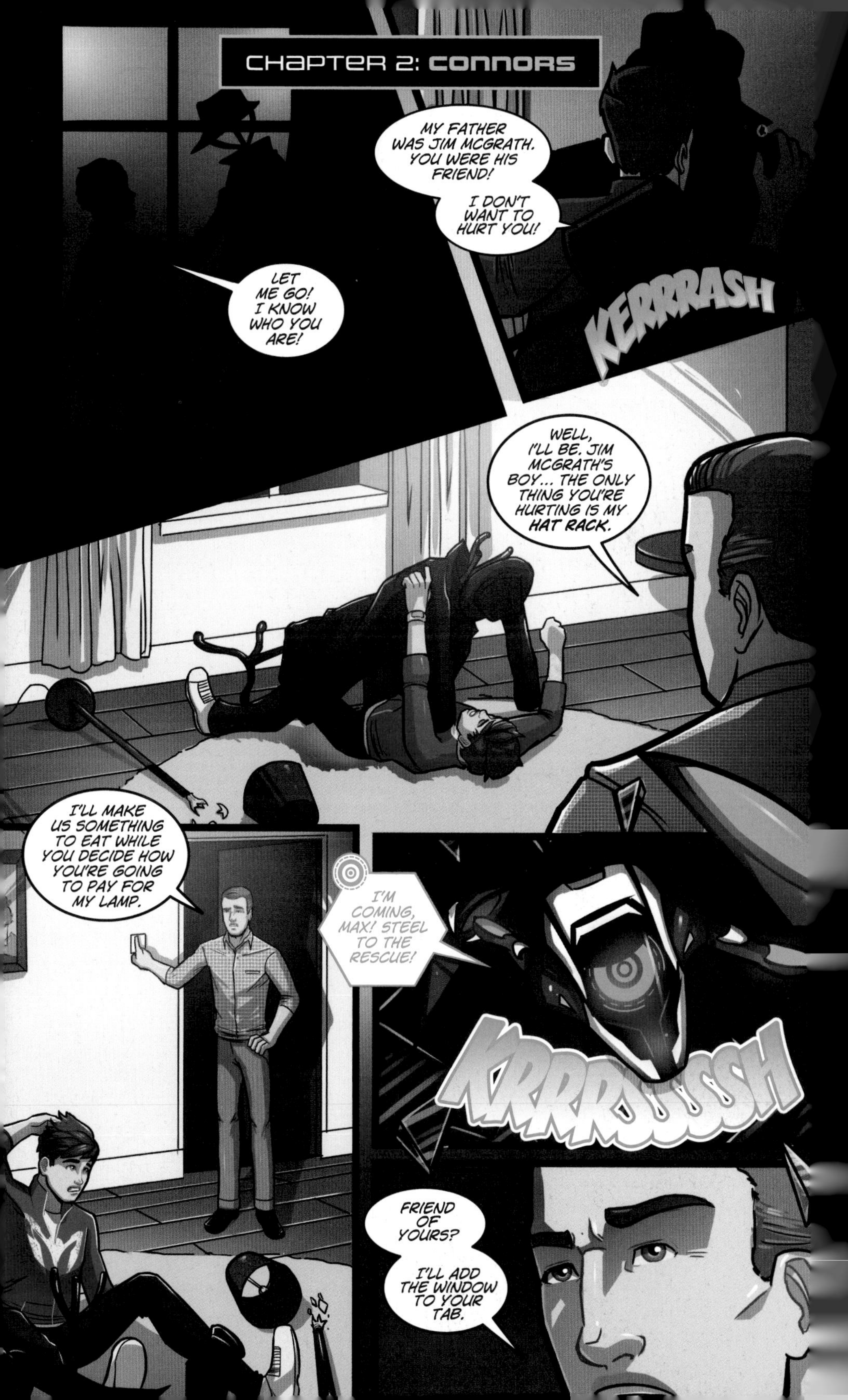
MY FATHER WAS JIM MCGRATH. YOU WERE HIS FRIEND!
I DON'T WANT TO HURT YOU!
LET ME GO! I KNOW WHO YOU ARE!
KERRRASH
WELL, I'LL BE. JIM MCGRATH'S BOY... THE ONLY THING YOU'RE HURTING IS MY HAT RACK.
I'LL MAKE US SOMETHING TO EAT WHILE YOU DECIDE HOW YOU'RE GOING TO PAY FOR MY LAMP.
I'M COMING, MAX! STEEL TO THE RESCUE!
KRRRSSSSH
FRIEND OF YOURS?
I'LL ADD THE WINDOW TO YOUR TAB.

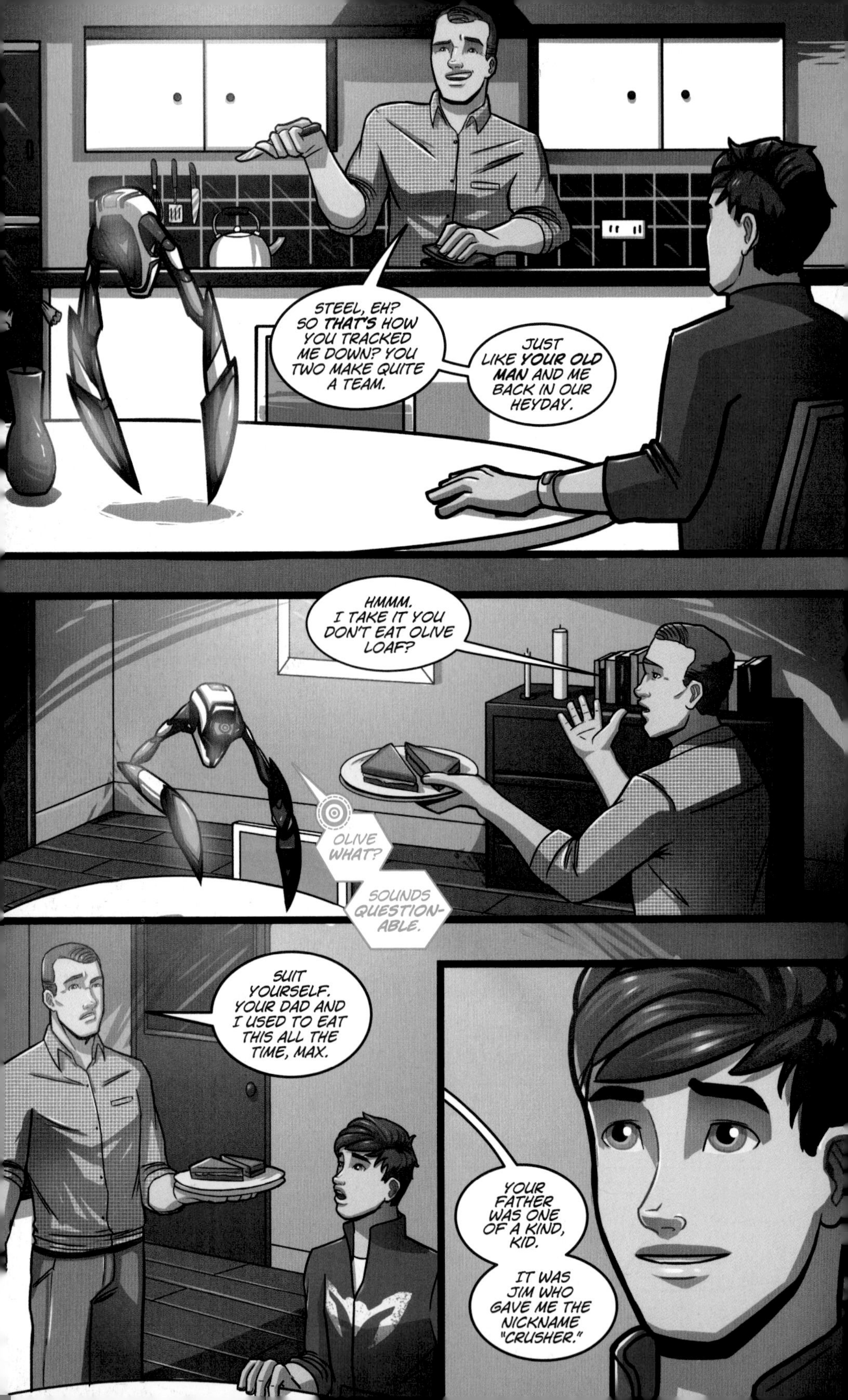

STEEL, EH? SO THAT'S HOW YOU TRACKED ME DOWN? YOU TWO MAKE QUITE A TEAM.
JUST LIKE YOUR OLD MAN AND ME BACK IN OUR HEYDAY.
HMMM. I TAKE IT YOU DON'T EAT OLIVE LOAF?
OLIVE WHAT?
SOUNDS QUESTION-ABLE.
SUIT YOURSELF. YOUR DAD AND I USED TO EAT THIS ALL THE TIME, MAX.
YOUR FATHER WAS ONE OF A KIND, KID.
IT WAS JIM WHO GAVE ME THE NICKNAME "CRUSHER."

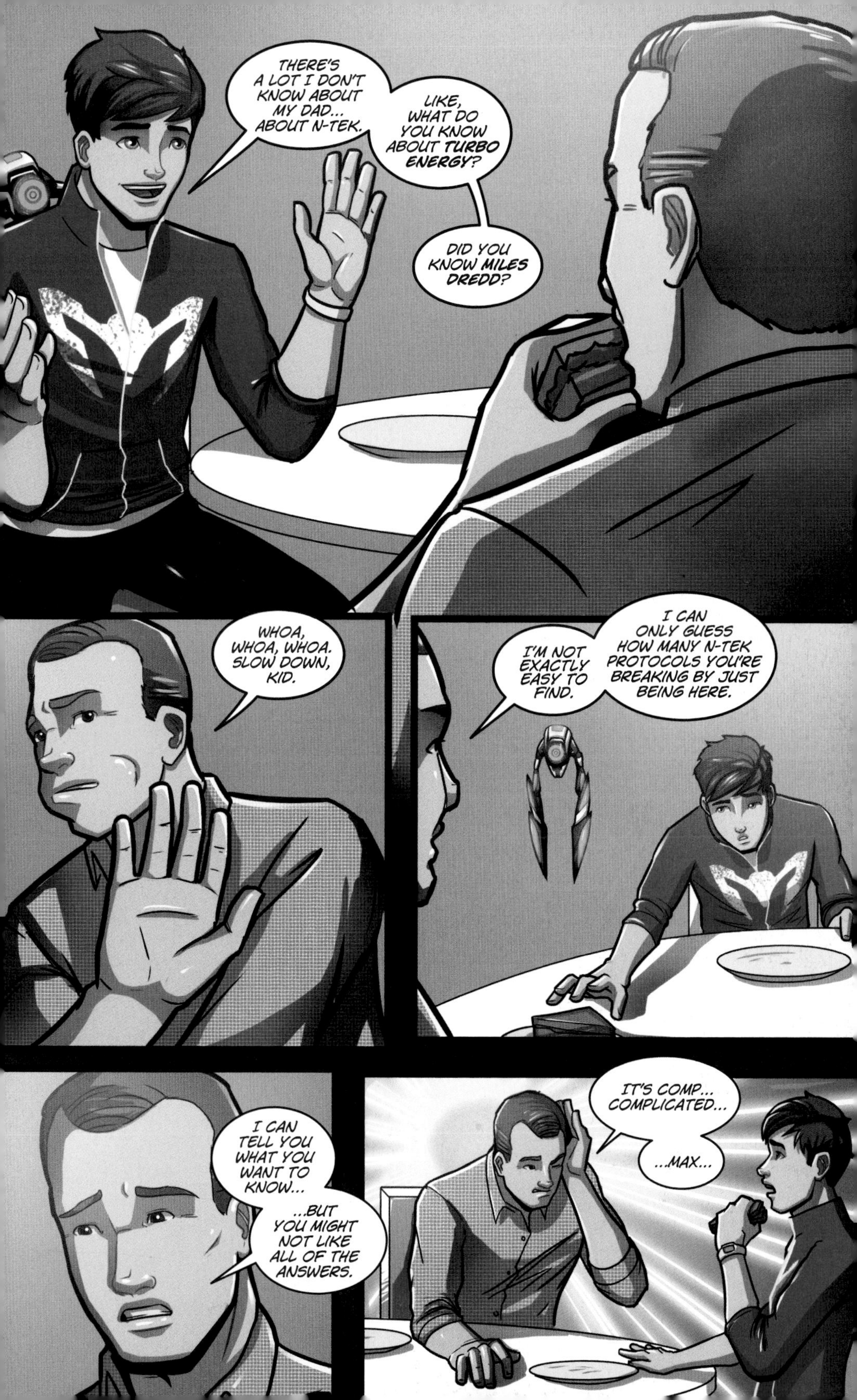
THERE'S A LOT I DON'T KNOW ABOUT MY DAD... ABOUT N-TEK.
LIKE, WHAT DO YOU KNOW ABOUT TURBO ENERGY?
DID YOU KNOW MILES DREDD?
WHOA, WHOA, WHOA. SLOW DOWN, KID.
I'M NOT EXACTLY EASY TO FIND.
I CAN ONLY GUESS HOW MANY N-TEK PROTOCOLS YOU'RE BREAKING BY JUST BEING HERE.
I CAN TELL YOU WHAT YOU WANT TO KNOW...
...BUT YOU MIGHT NOT LIKE ALL OF THE ANSWERS.
IT'S COMP... COMPLICATED...
...MAX...

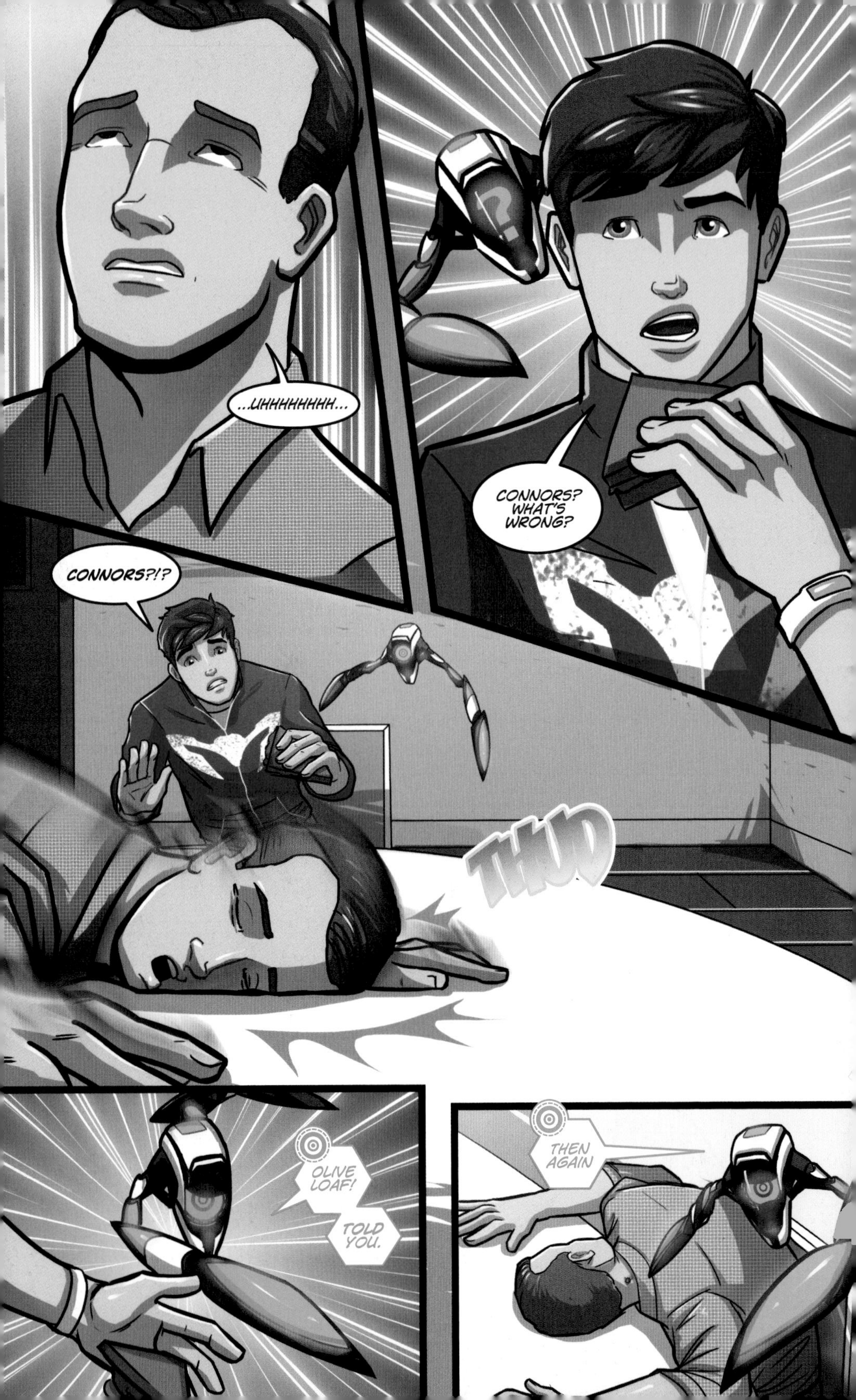
...UHHHHHHHH...
CONNORS? WHAT'S WRONG?
CONNORS?!?
THUD
OLIVE LOAF!
TOLD YOU.
THEN AGAIN

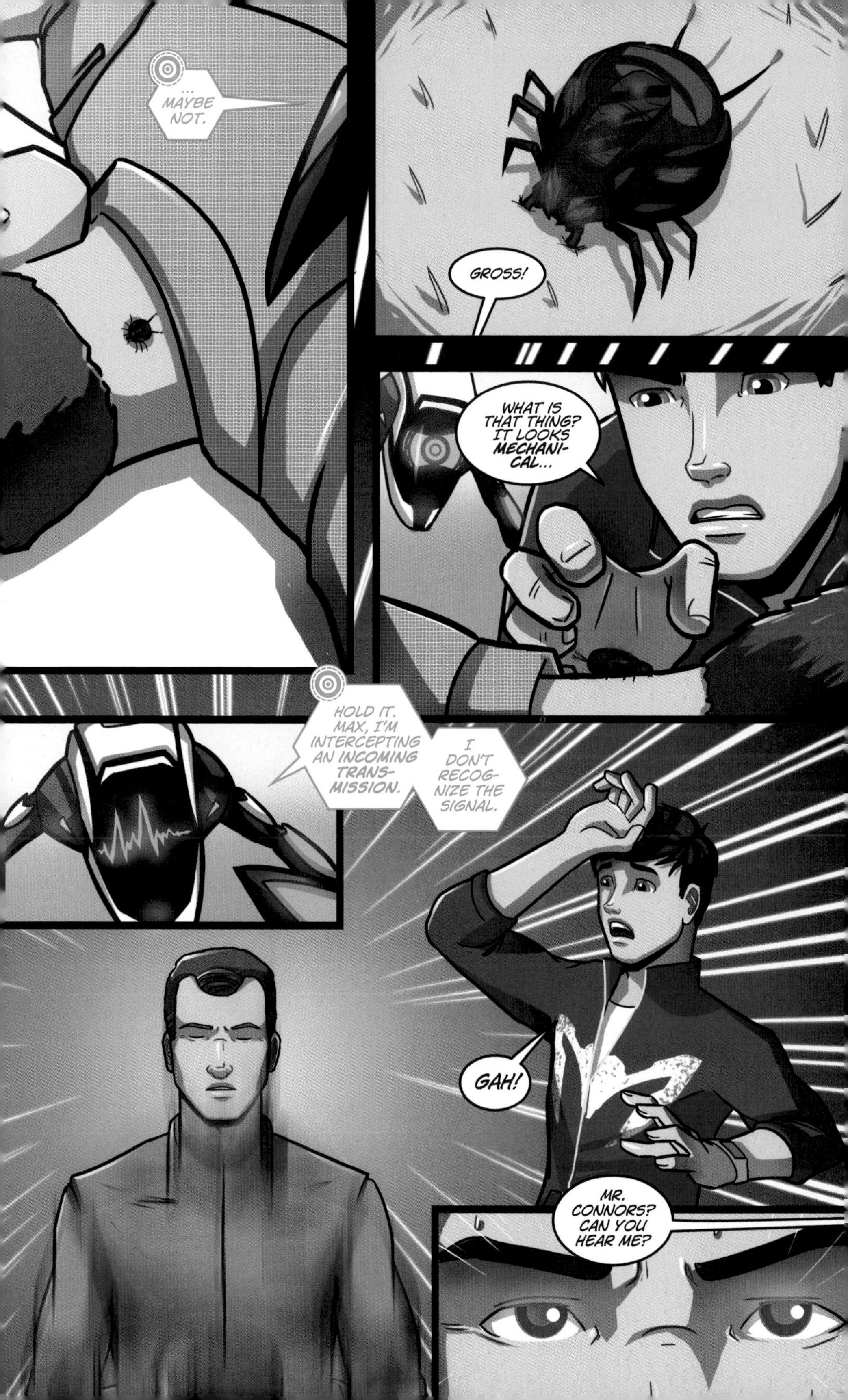
...
MAYBE NOT.
GROSS!
WHAT IS THAT THING? IT LOOKS MECHANICAL...
HOLD IT. MAX, I'M INTERCEPTING AN INCOMING TRANSMISSION.
I DON'T RECOGNIZE THE SIGNAL.
GAH!
MR. CONNORS? CAN YOU HEAR ME?

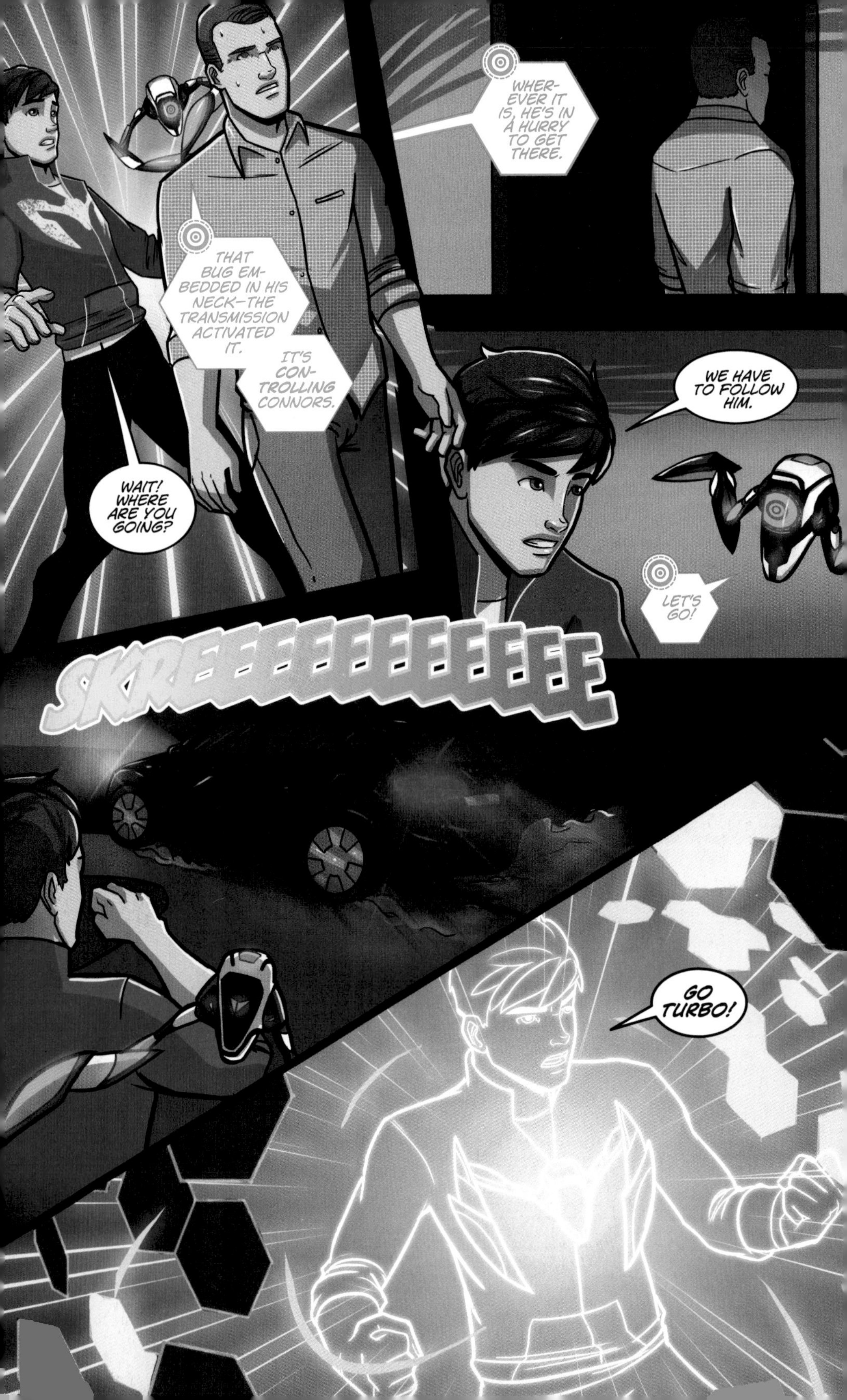
WHER-EVER IT IS, HE'S IN A HURRY TO GET THERE.
THAT BUG EM-BEDDED IN HIS NECK—THE TRANSMISSION ACTIVATED IT.
IT'S CON-TROLLING CONNORS.
WAIT! WHERE ARE YOU GOING?
WE HAVE TO FOLLOW HIM.
LET'S GO!
SKREEEEEEEEEEEE
GO TURBO!

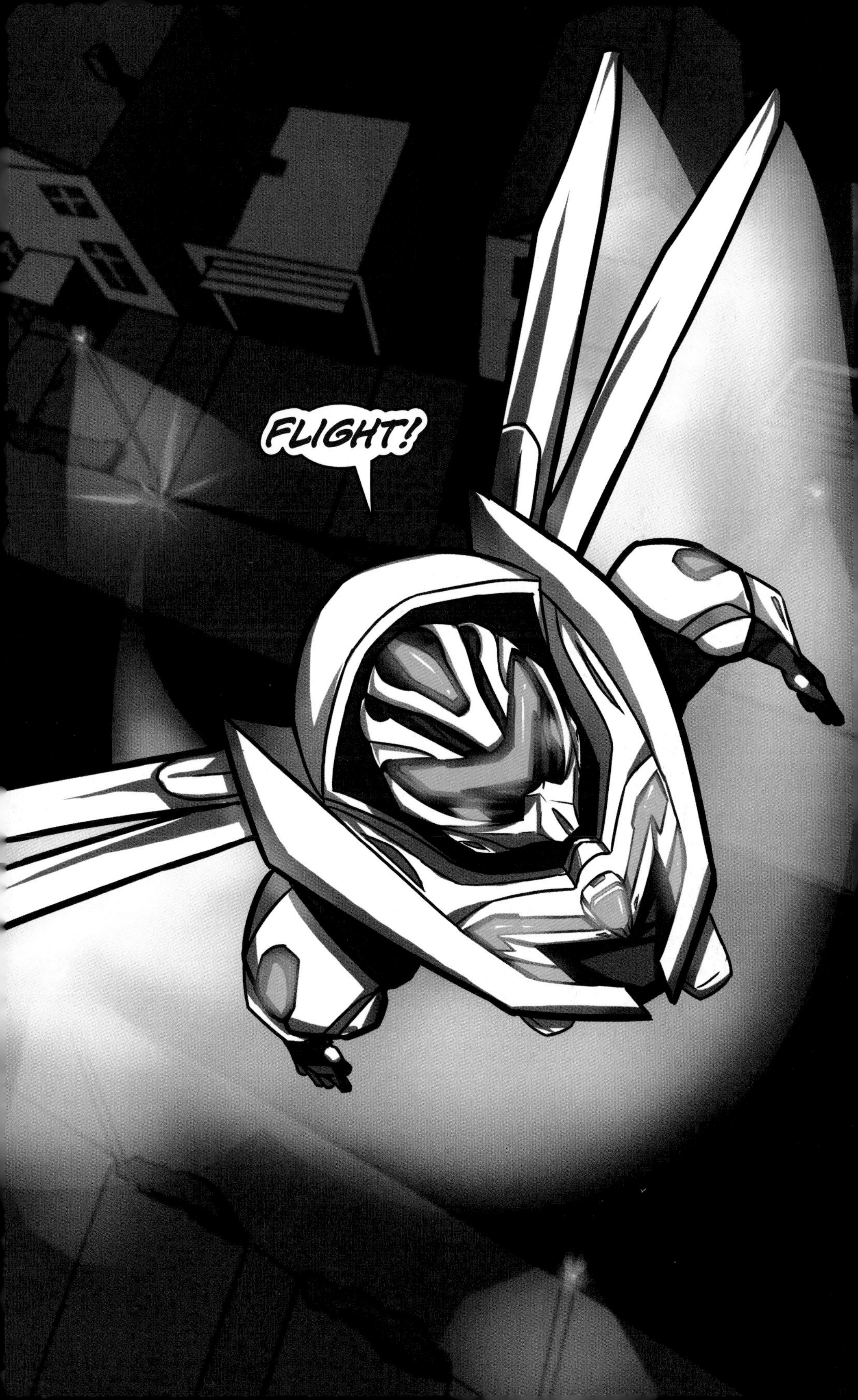
FLIGHT!

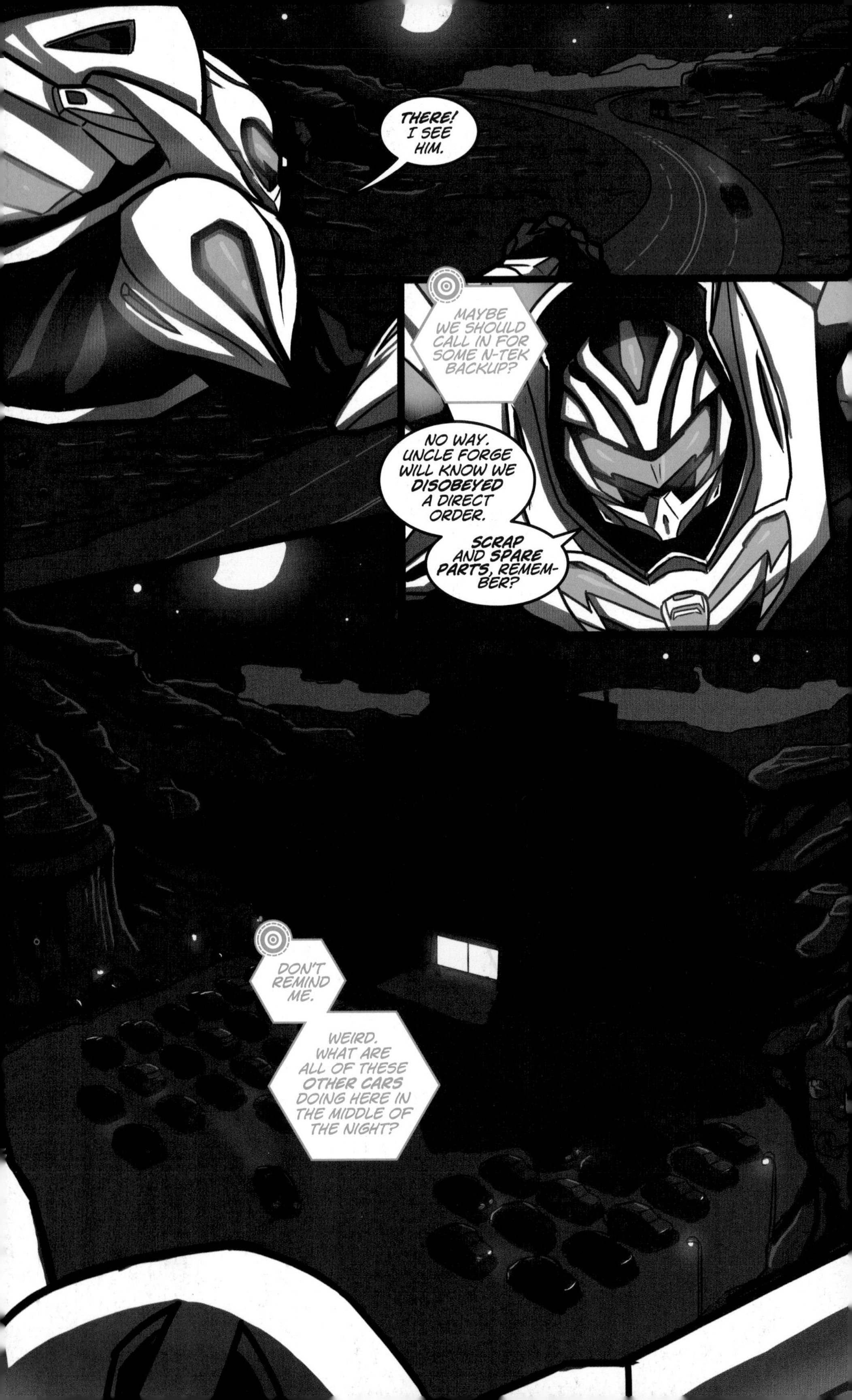
THERE! I SEE HIM.
MAYBE WE SHOULD CALL IN FOR SOME N-TEK BACKUP?
NO WAY. UNCLE FORGE WILL KNOW WE DISOBEYED A DIRECT ORDER.
SCRAP AND SPARE PARTS, REMEMBER?
DON'T REMIND ME.
WEIRD. WHAT ARE ALL OF THESE OTHER CARS DOING HERE IN THE MIDDLE OF THE NIGHT?

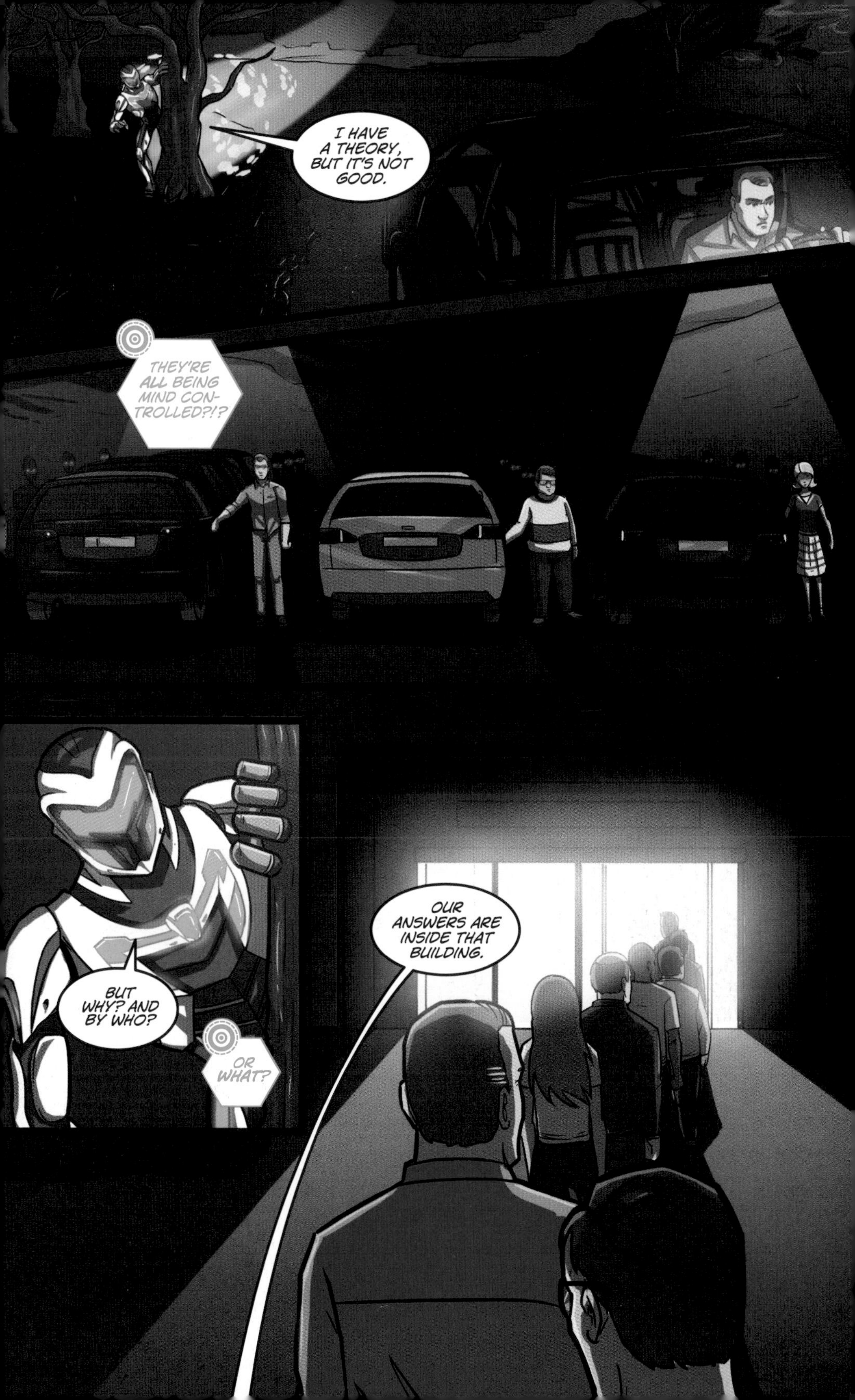
I HAVE A THEORY, BUT IT'S NOT GOOD.
THEY'RE ALL BEING MIND CONTROLLED?!?
BUT WHY? AND BY WHO?
OR WHAT?
OUR ANSWERS ARE INSIDE THAT BUILDING.

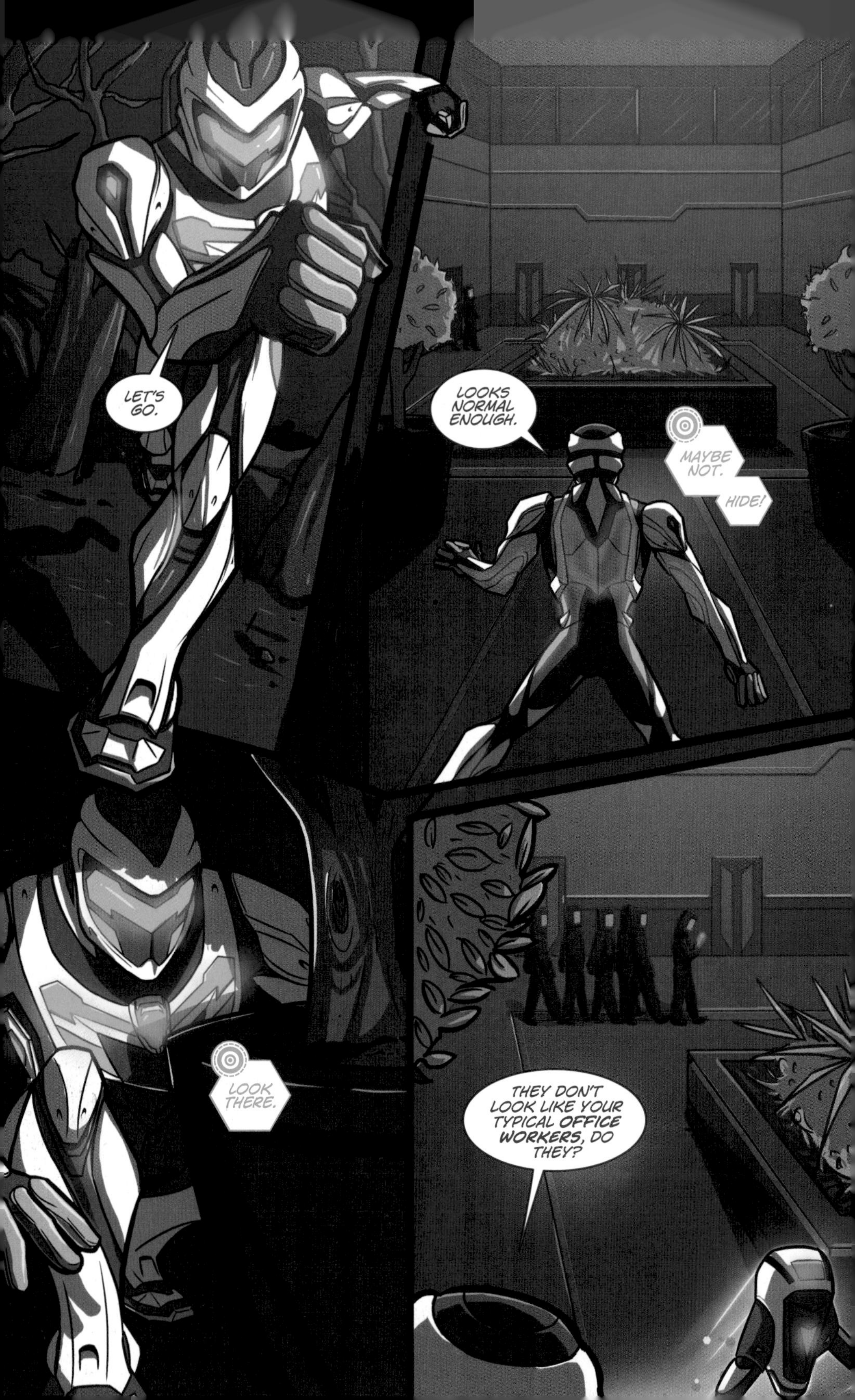
LET'S GO.
LOOKS NORMAL ENOUGH.
MAYBE NOT.
HIDE!
LOOK THERE.
THEY DON'T LOOK LIKE YOUR TYPICAL OFFICE WORKERS, DO THEY?

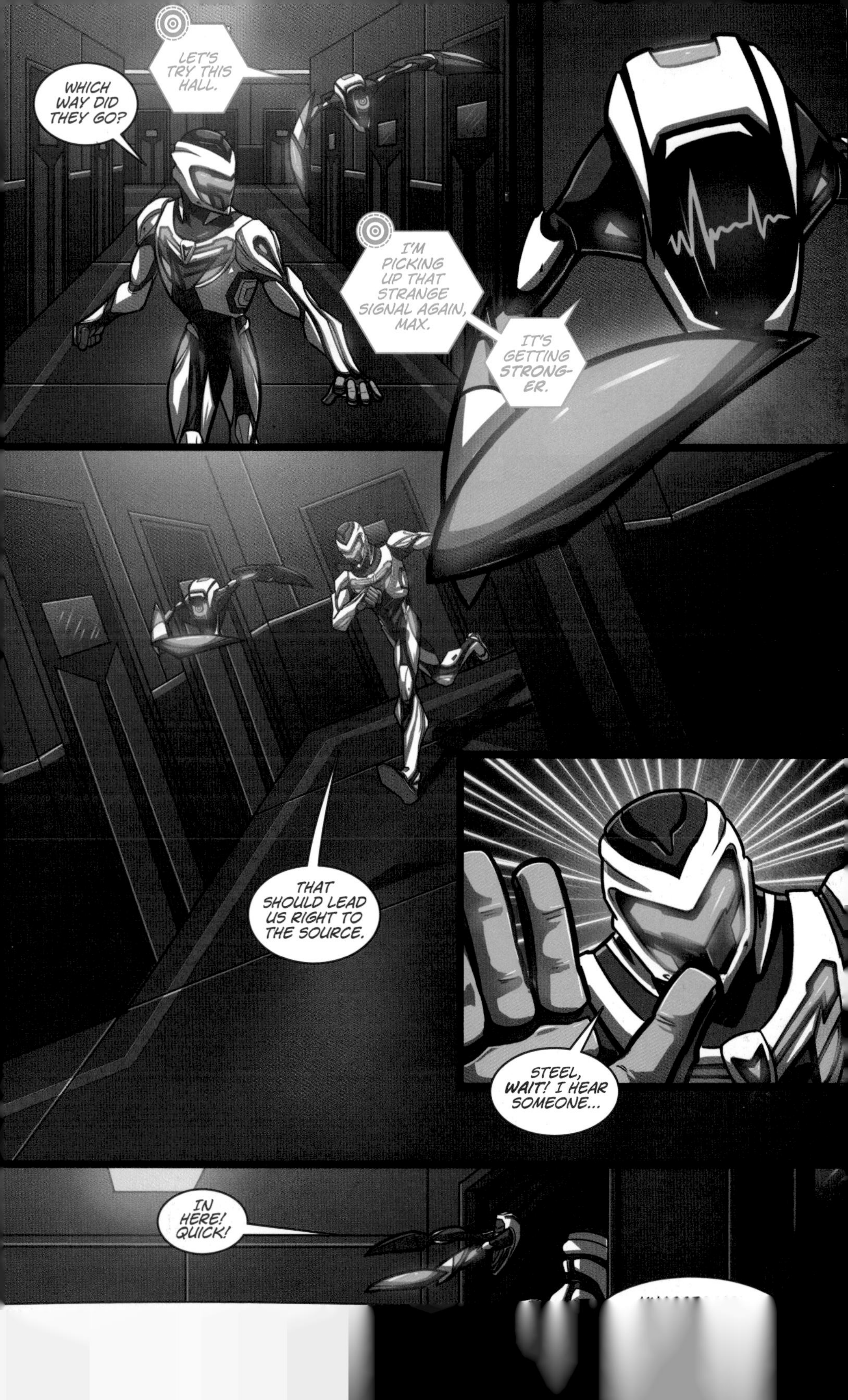
WHICH WAY DID THEY GO?
LET'S TRY THIS HALL.
I'M PICKING UP THAT STRANGE SIGNAL AGAIN, MAX.
IT'S GETTING STRONGER.
THAT SHOULD LEAD US RIGHT TO THE SOURCE.
STEEL, WAIT! I HEAR SOMEONE...
IN HERE! QUICK!

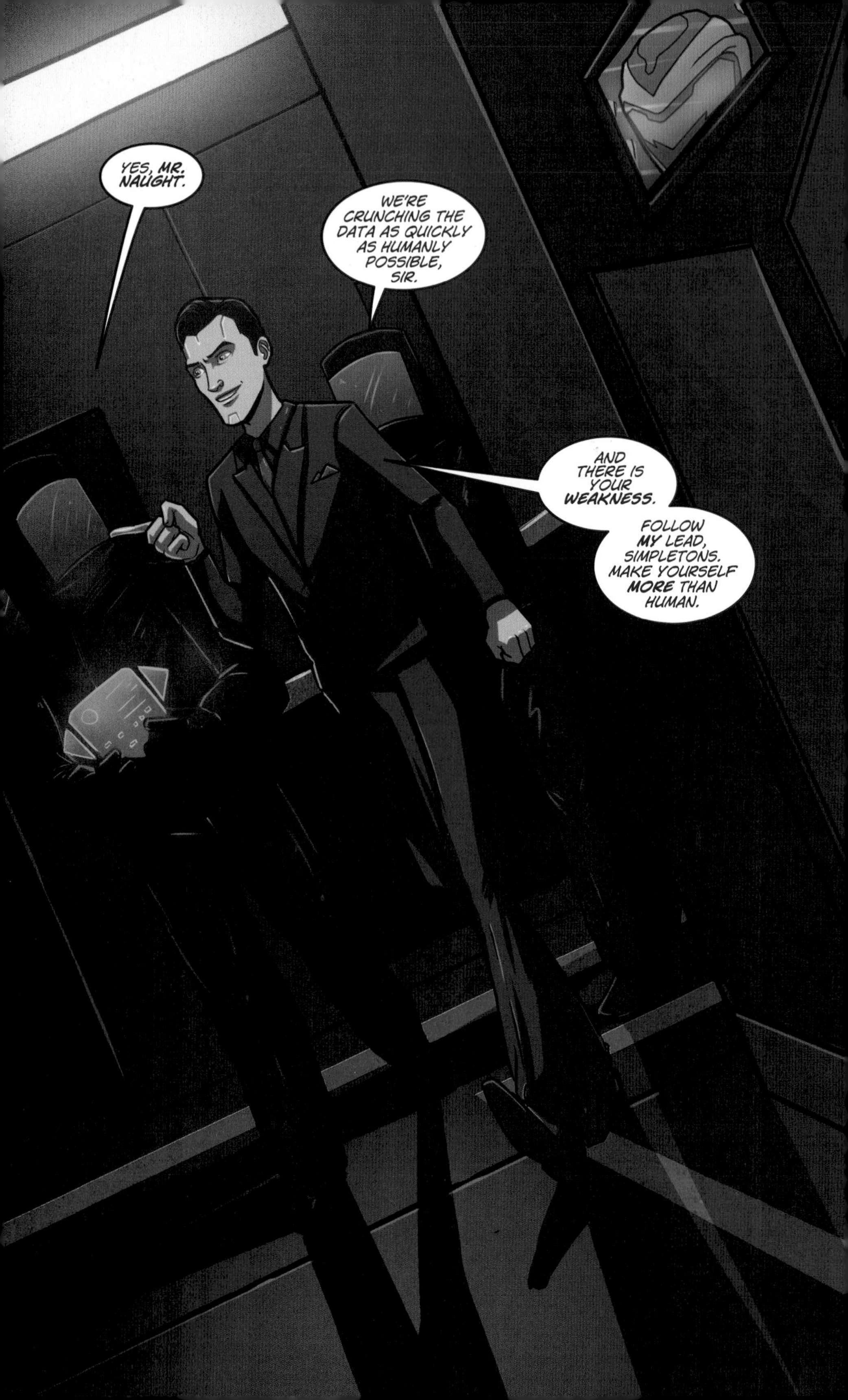
YES, MR. NAUGHT.
WE'RE CRUNCHING THE DATA AS QUICKLY AS HUMANLY POSSIBLE, SIR.
AND THERE IS YOUR WEAKNESS.
FOLLOW MY LEAD, SIMPLETONS. MAKE YOURSELF MORE THAN HUMAN.

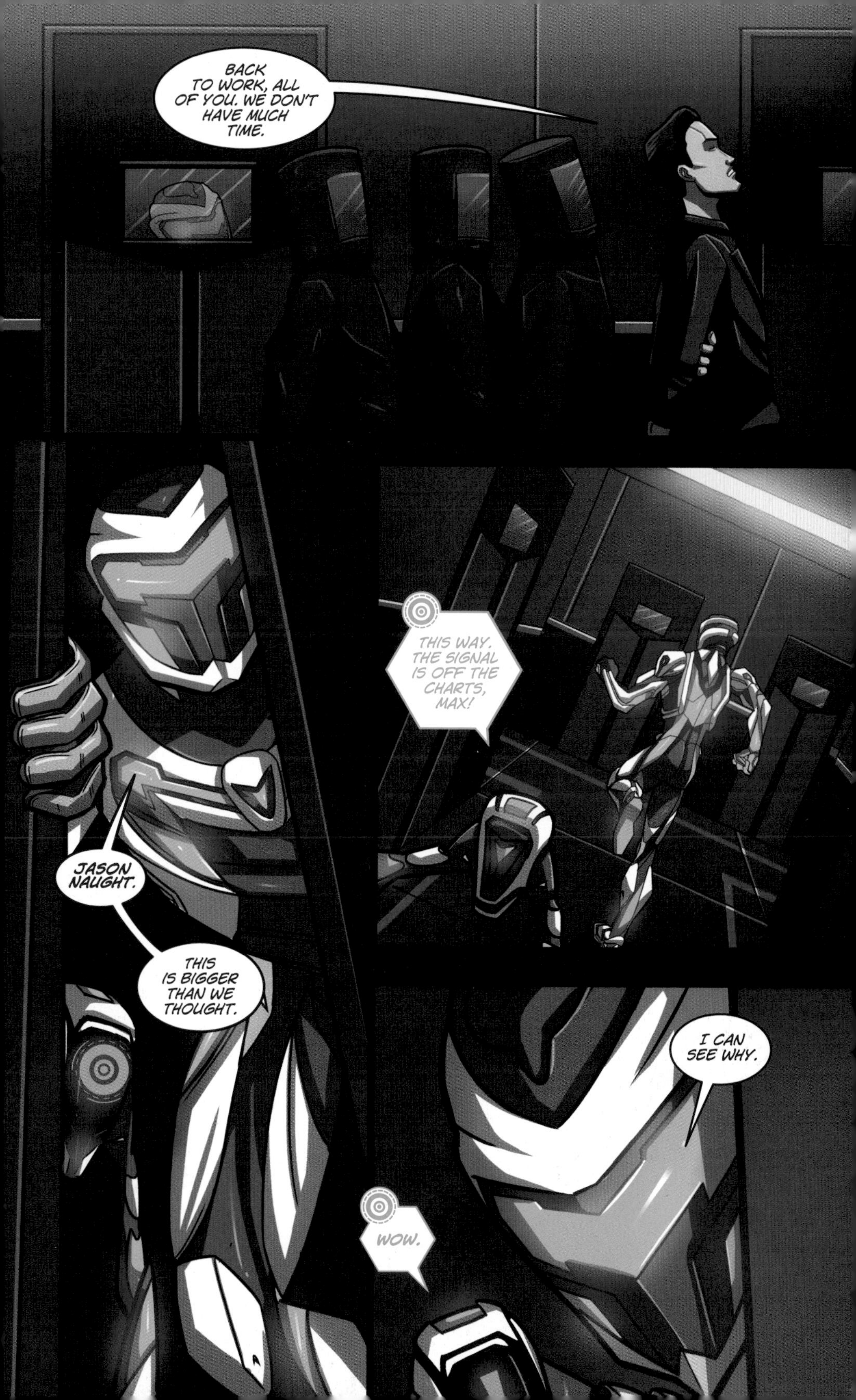
BACK TO WORK, ALL OF YOU. WE DON'T HAVE MUCH TIME.
JASON NAUGHT.
THIS IS BIGGER THAN WE THOUGHT.
THIS WAY. THE SIGNAL IS OFF THE CHARTS, MAX!
I CAN SEE WHY.
WOW.

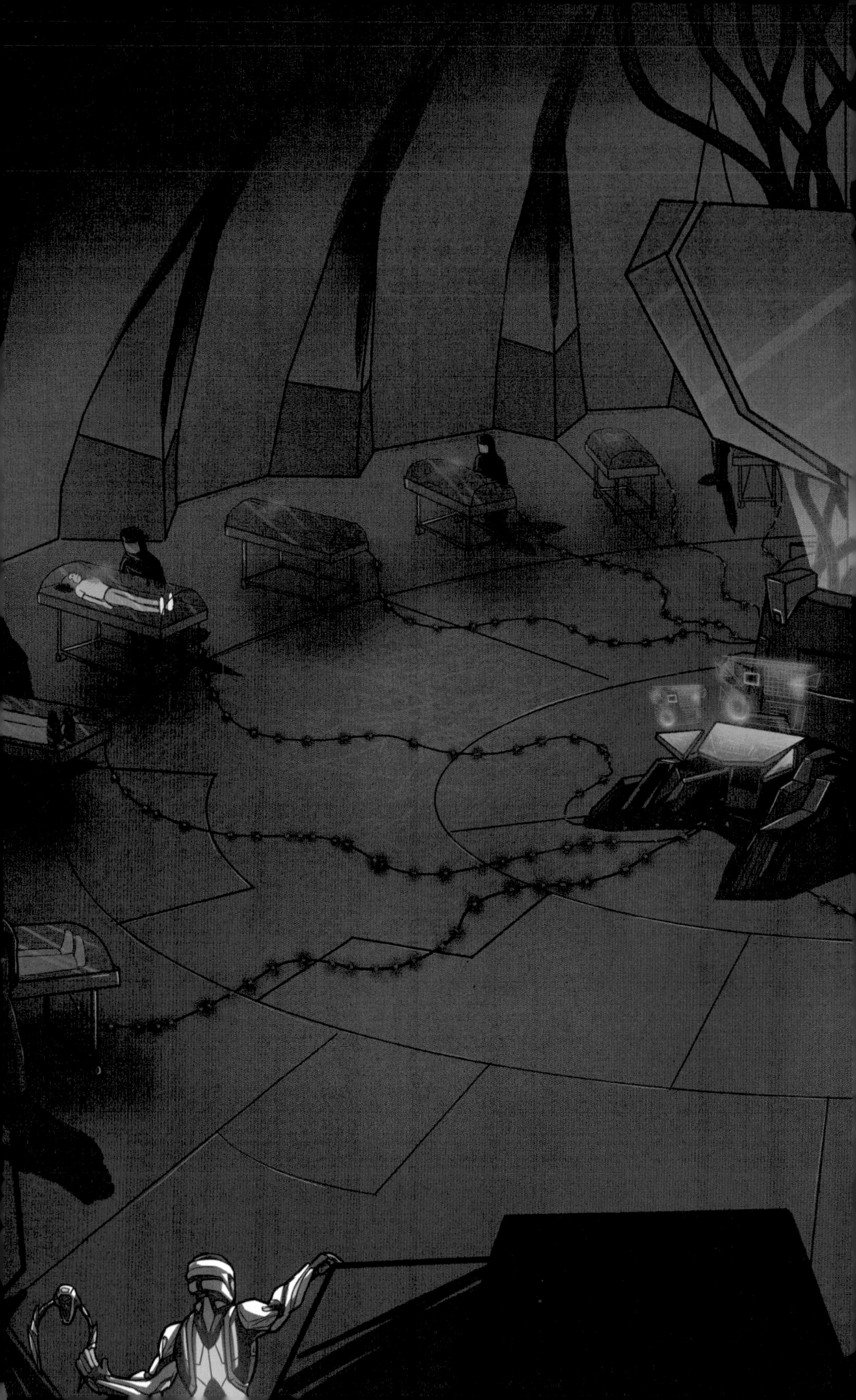

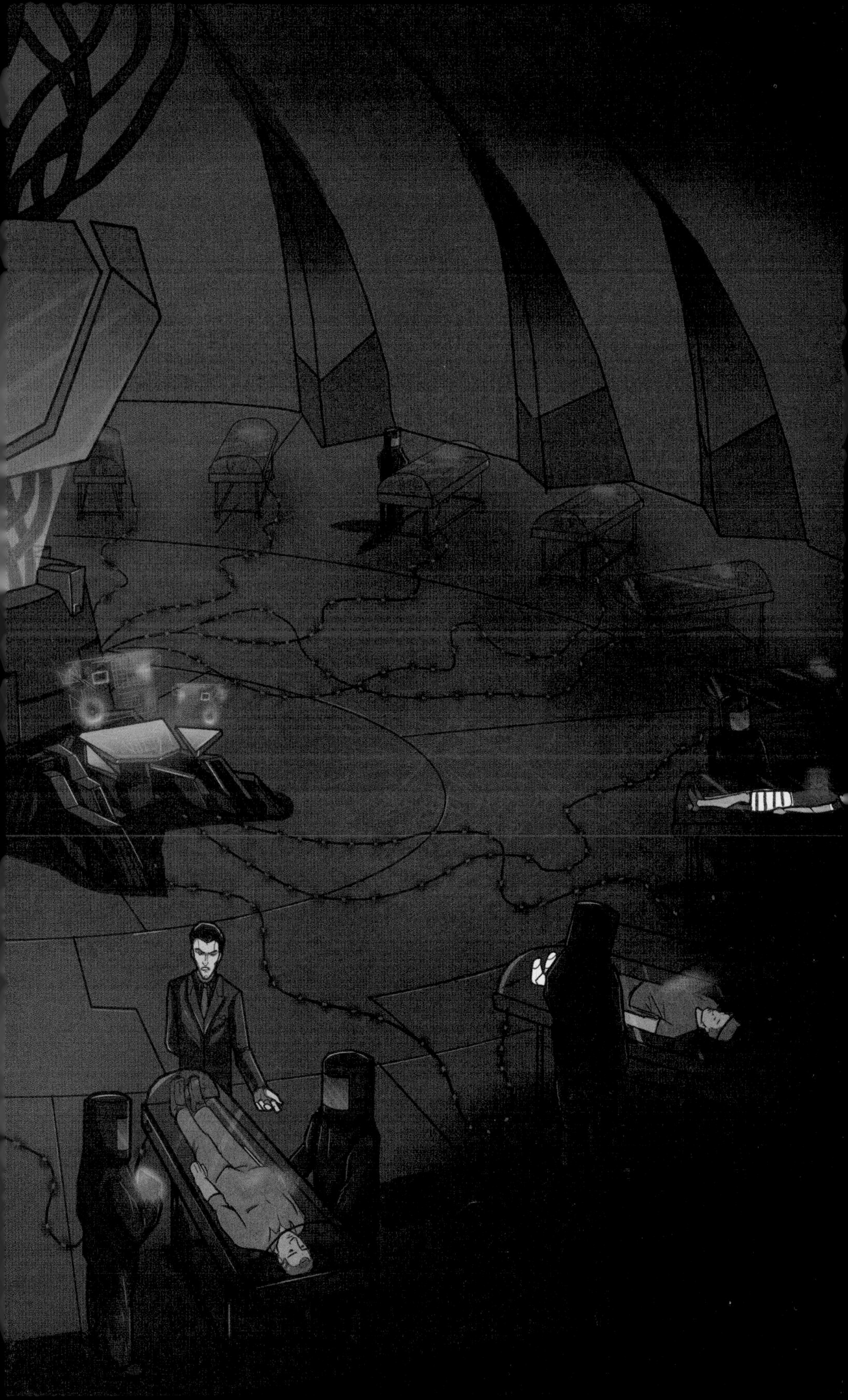

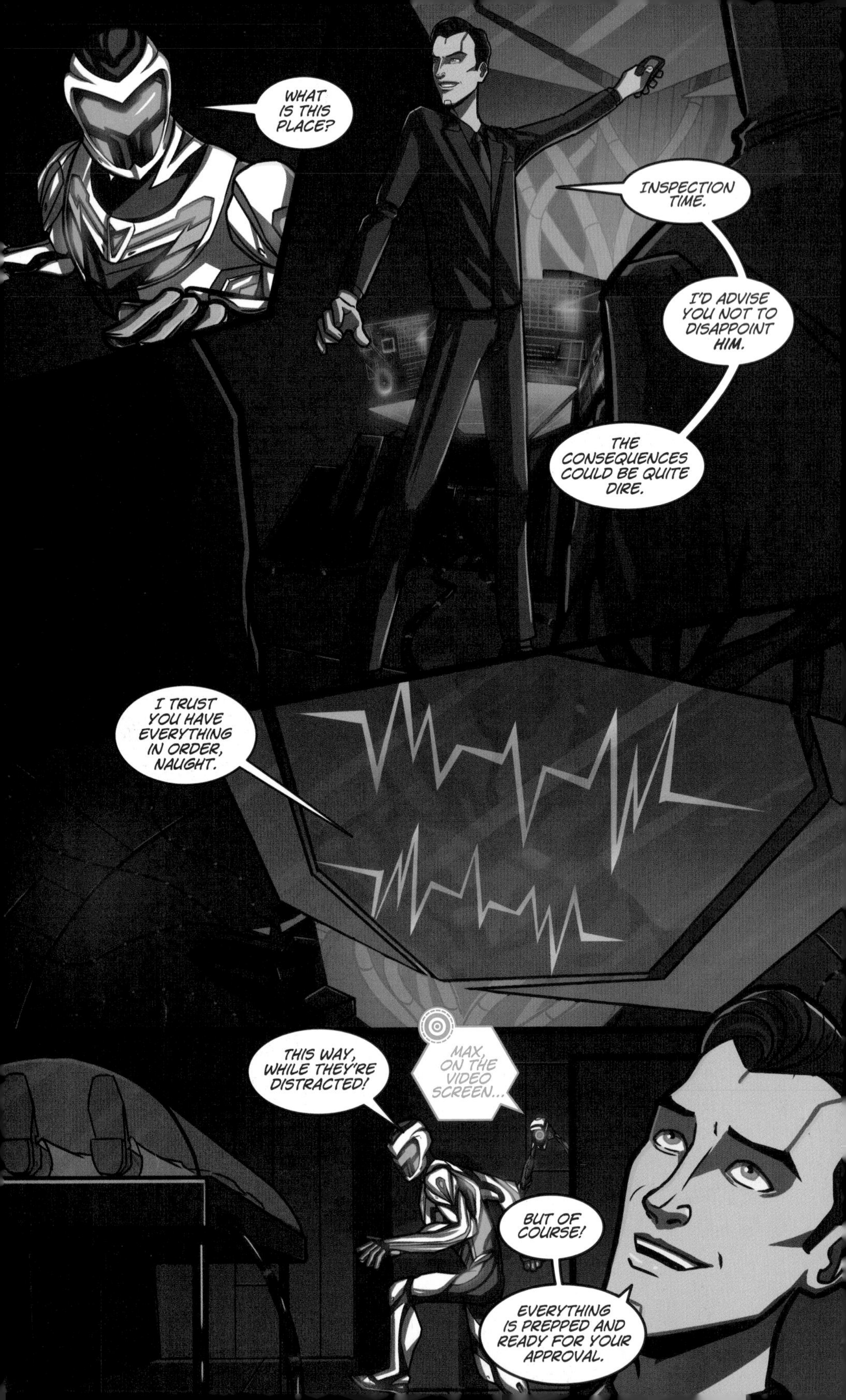
WHAT IS THIS PLACE?
INSPECTION TIME.
I'D ADVISE YOU NOT TO DISAPPOINT HIM.
THE CONSEQUENCES COULD BE QUITE DIRE.
I TRUST YOU HAVE EVERYTHING IN ORDER, NAUGHT.
THIS WAY, WHILE THEY'RE DISTRACTED!
MAX, ON THE VIDEO SCREEN...
BUT OF COURSE!
EVERYTHING IS PREPPED AND READY FOR YOUR APPROVAL.

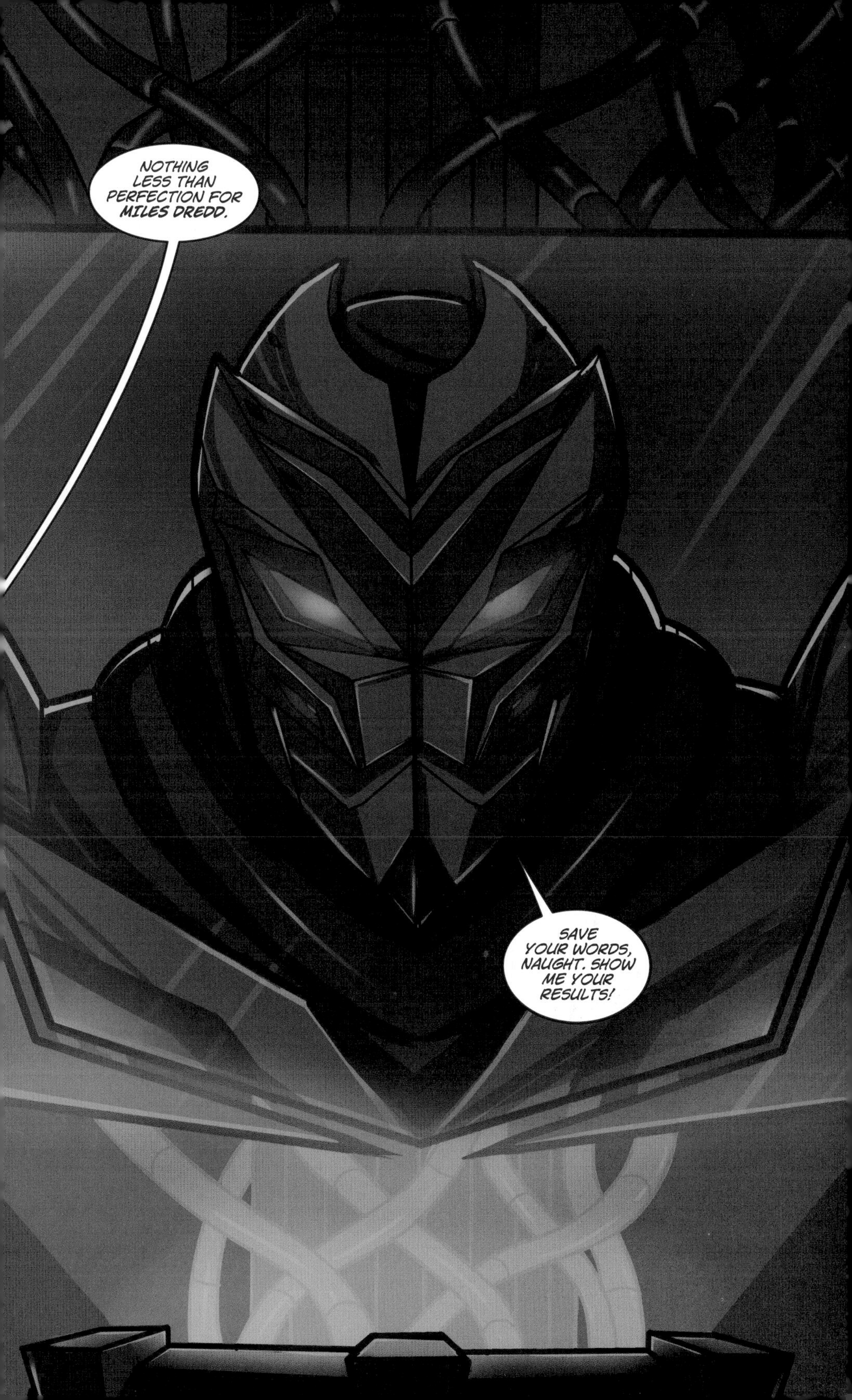
NOTHING LESS THAN PERFECTION FOR MILES DREDD.
SAVE YOUR WORDS, NAUGHT. SHOW ME YOUR RESULTS!

CHAPTER 3: DREDD'S DRONES

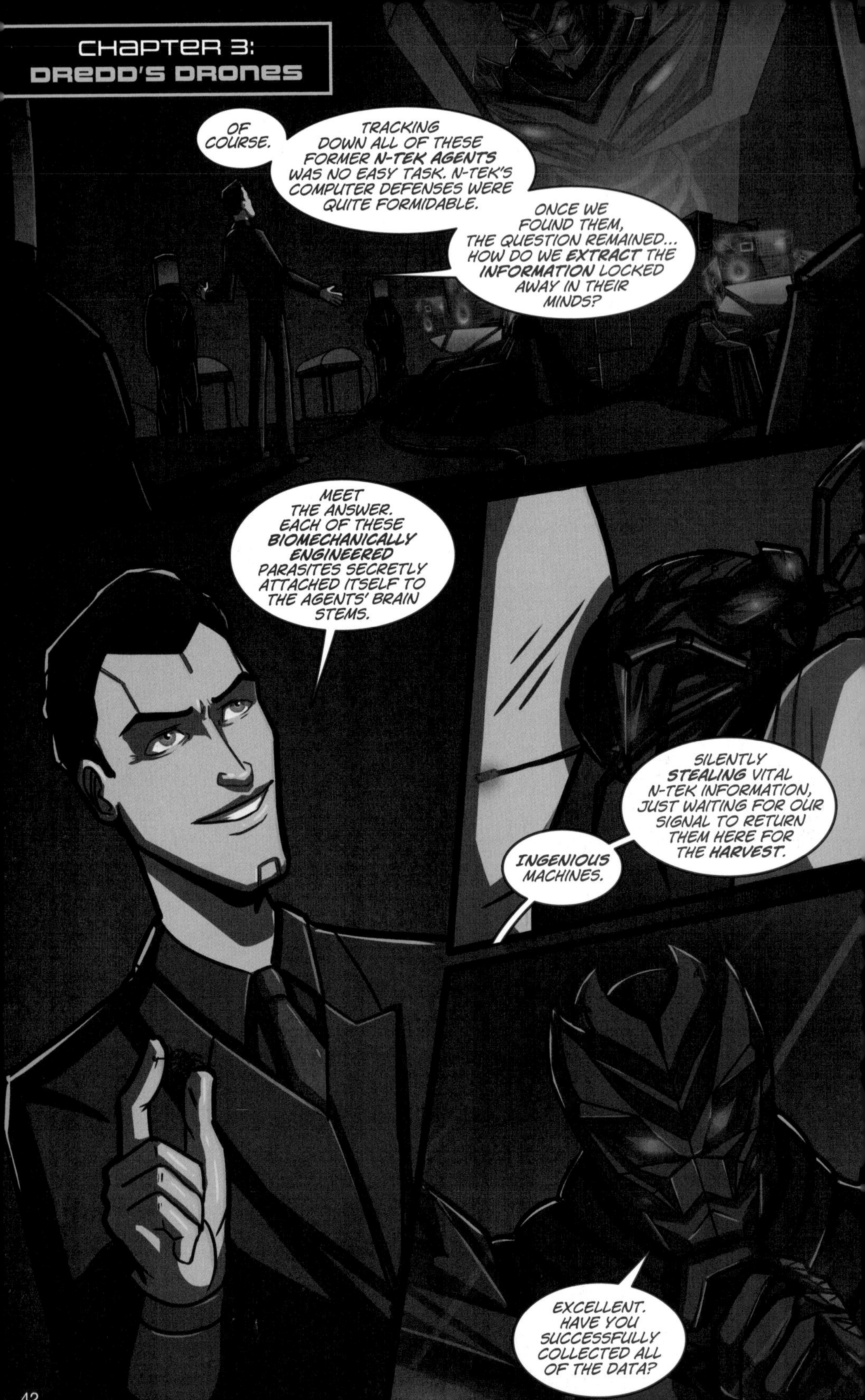

OF COURSE.
TRACKING DOWN ALL OF THESE FORMER N-TEK AGENTS WAS NO EASY TASK. N-TEK'S COMPUTER DEFENSES WERE QUITE FORMIDABLE.
ONCE WE FOUND THEM, THE QUESTION REMAINED... HOW DO WE EXTRACT THE INFORMATION LOCKED AWAY IN THEIR MINDS?
MEET THE ANSWER. EACH OF THESE BIOMECHANICALLY ENGINEERED PARASITES SECRETLY ATTACHED ITSELF TO THE AGENTS' BRAIN STEMS.
SILENTLY STEALING VITAL N-TEK INFORMATION, JUST WAITING FOR OUR SIGNAL TO RETURN THEM HERE FOR THE HARVEST.
INGENIOUS MACHINES.
EXCELLENT. HAVE YOU SUCCESSFULLY COLLECTED ALL OF THE DATA?

WE HAVE. N-TEK'S SECRETS ARE YOURS.
ALL THAT REMAINS IS TO RECONSTRUCT THE DATA CONTAINED IN THE PARASITES.
WE CAN'T LET THEM STEAL THAT INFO, STEEL.
HEARD YOU GUYS HAD A BUG PROBLEM.

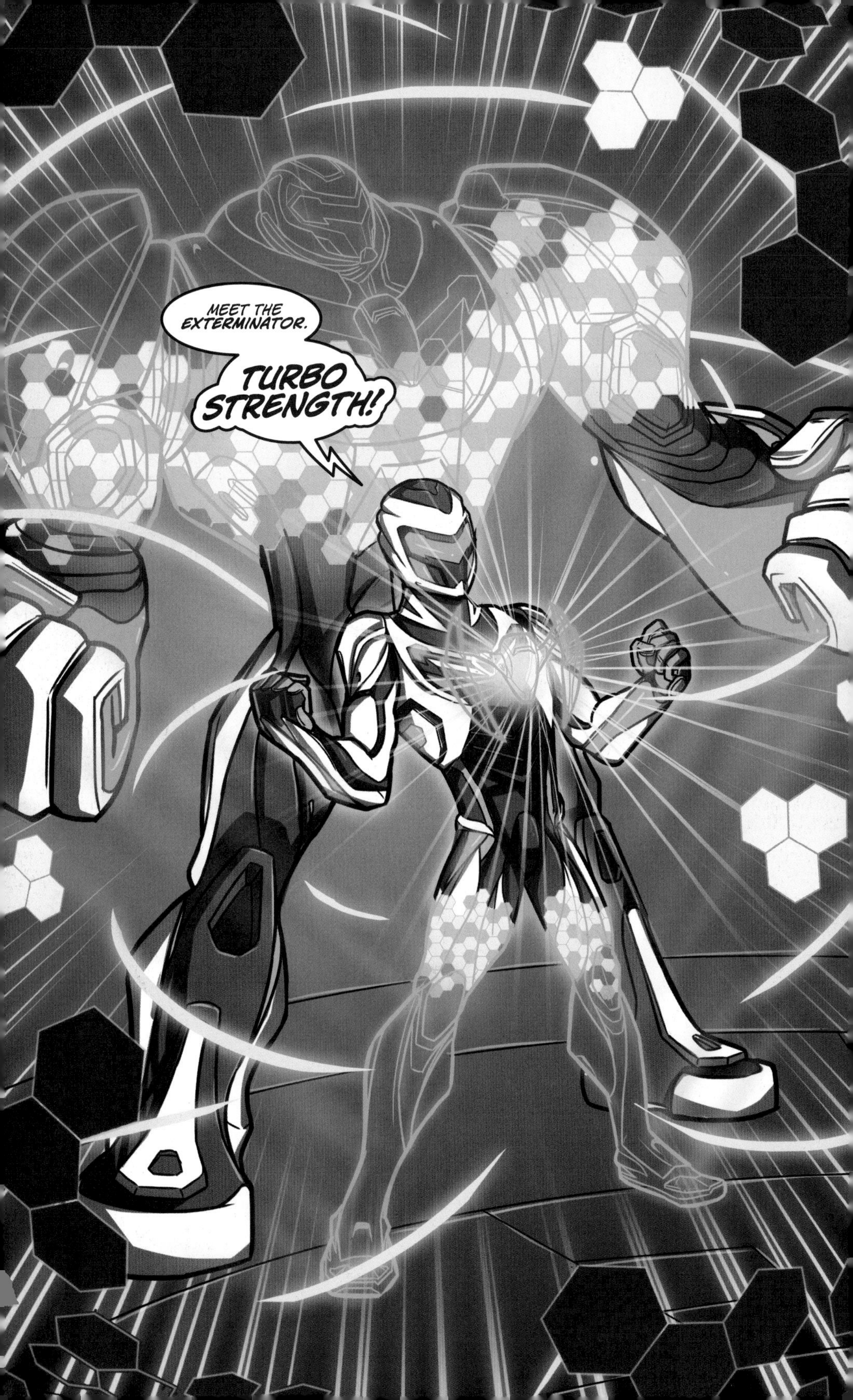
MEET THE EXTERMINATOR.
TURBO STRENGTH!

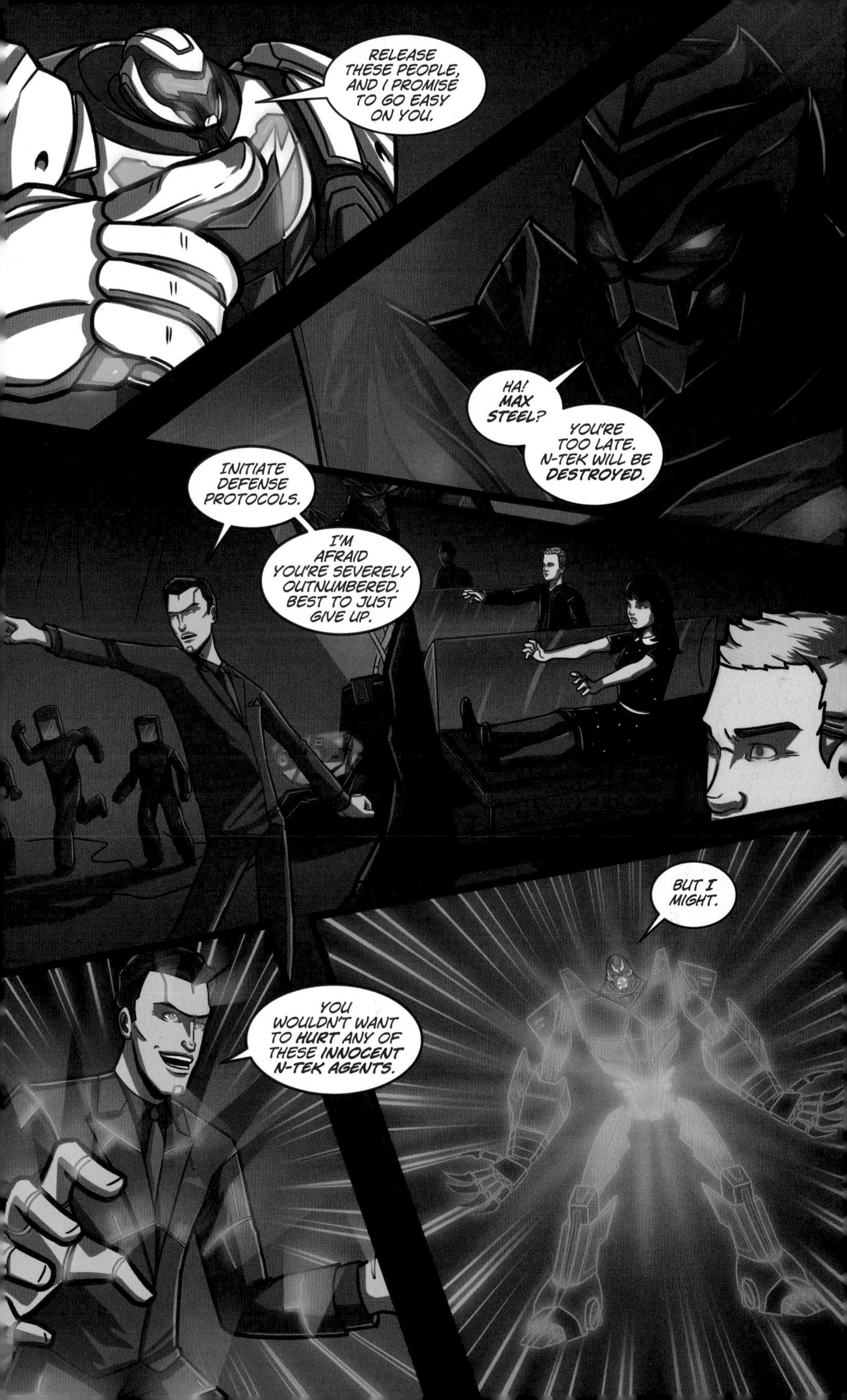
RELEASE THESE PEOPLE, AND I PROMISE TO GO EASY ON YOU.
HA! MAX STEEL?
YOU'RE TOO LATE. N-TEK WILL BE DESTROYED.
INITIATE DEFENSE PROTOCOLS.
I'M AFRAID YOU'RE SEVERELY OUTNUMBERED. BEST TO JUST GIVE UP.
YOU WOULDN'T WANT TO HURT ANY OF THESE INNOCENT N-TEK AGENTS.
BUT I MIGHT.

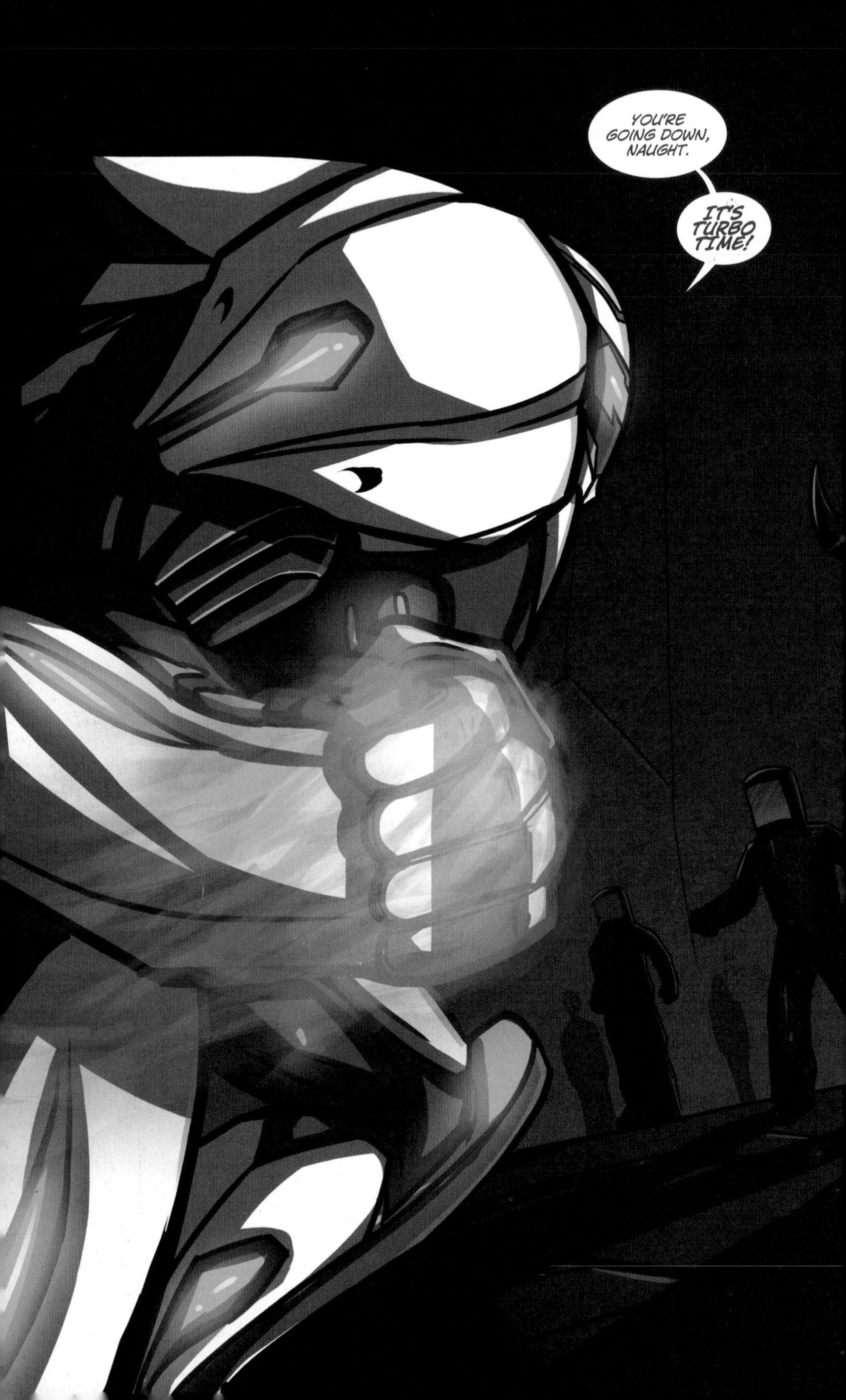
YOU'RE GOING DOWN, NAUGHT.
IT'S TURBO TIME!

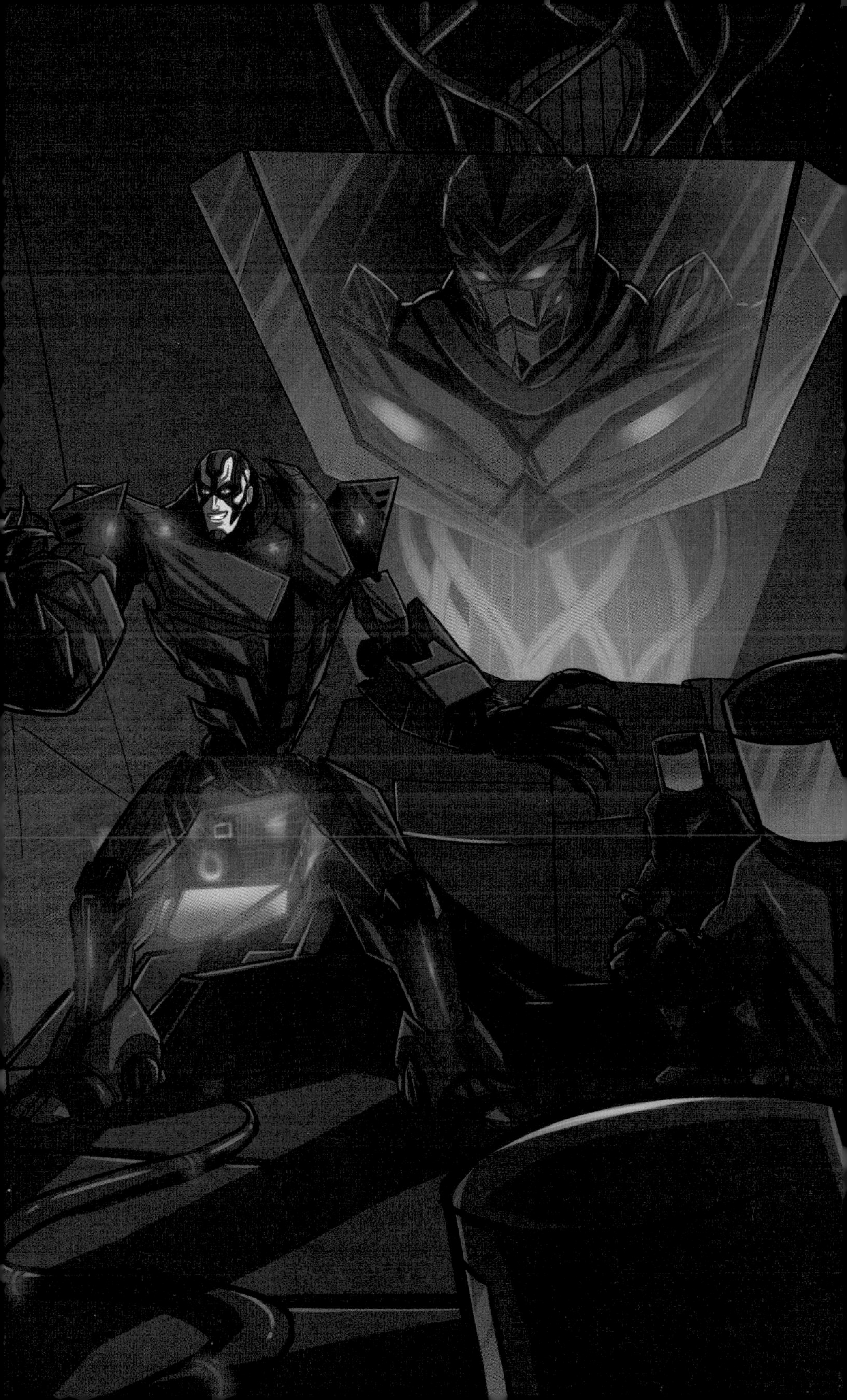

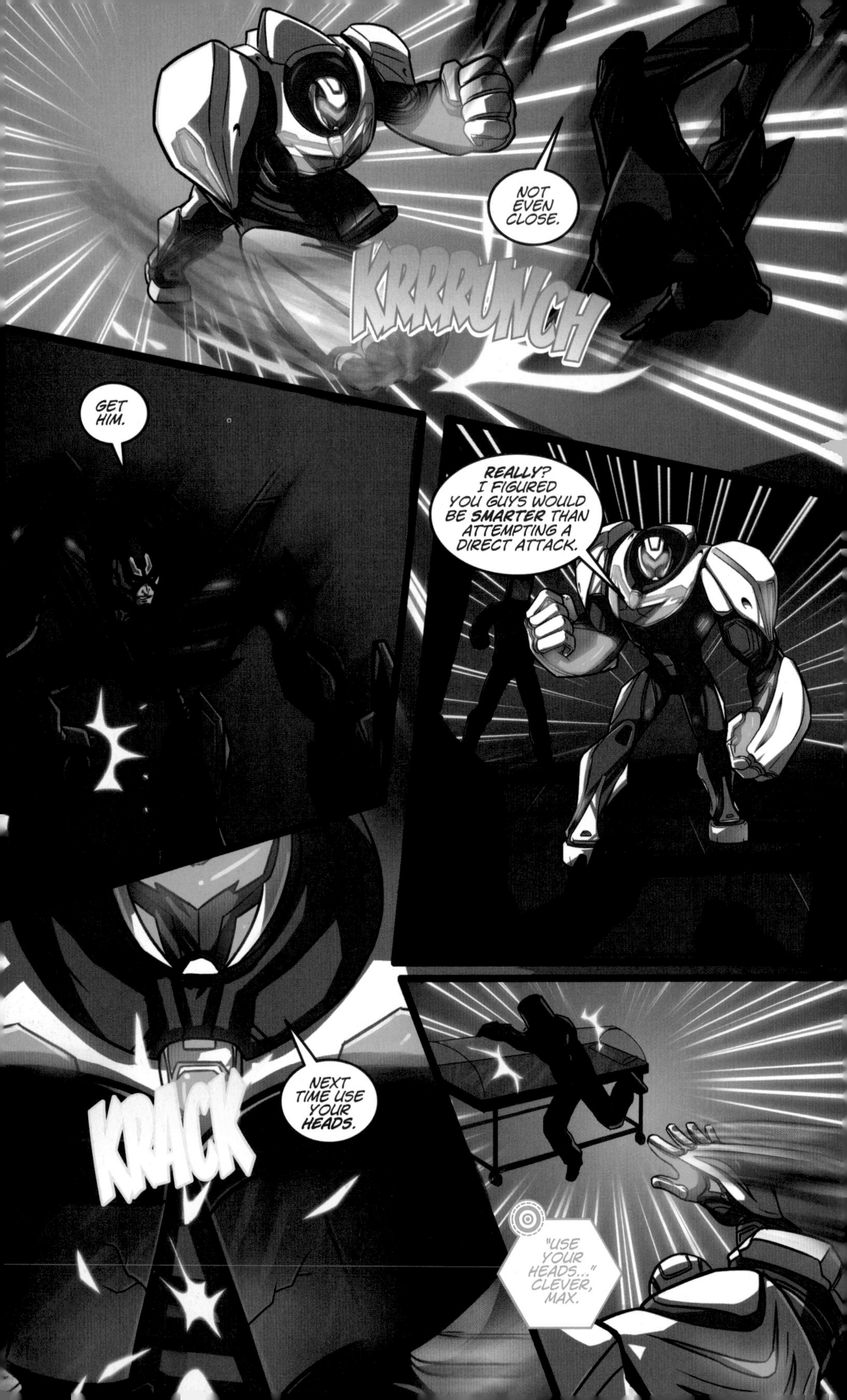
NOT EVEN CLOSE.
KRRRUNCH
GET HIM.
REALLY? I FIGURED YOU GUYS WOULD BE SMARTER THAN ATTEMPTING A DIRECT ATTACK.
KRACK
NEXT TIME USE YOUR HEADS.
"USE YOUR HEADS..." CLEVER, MAX.

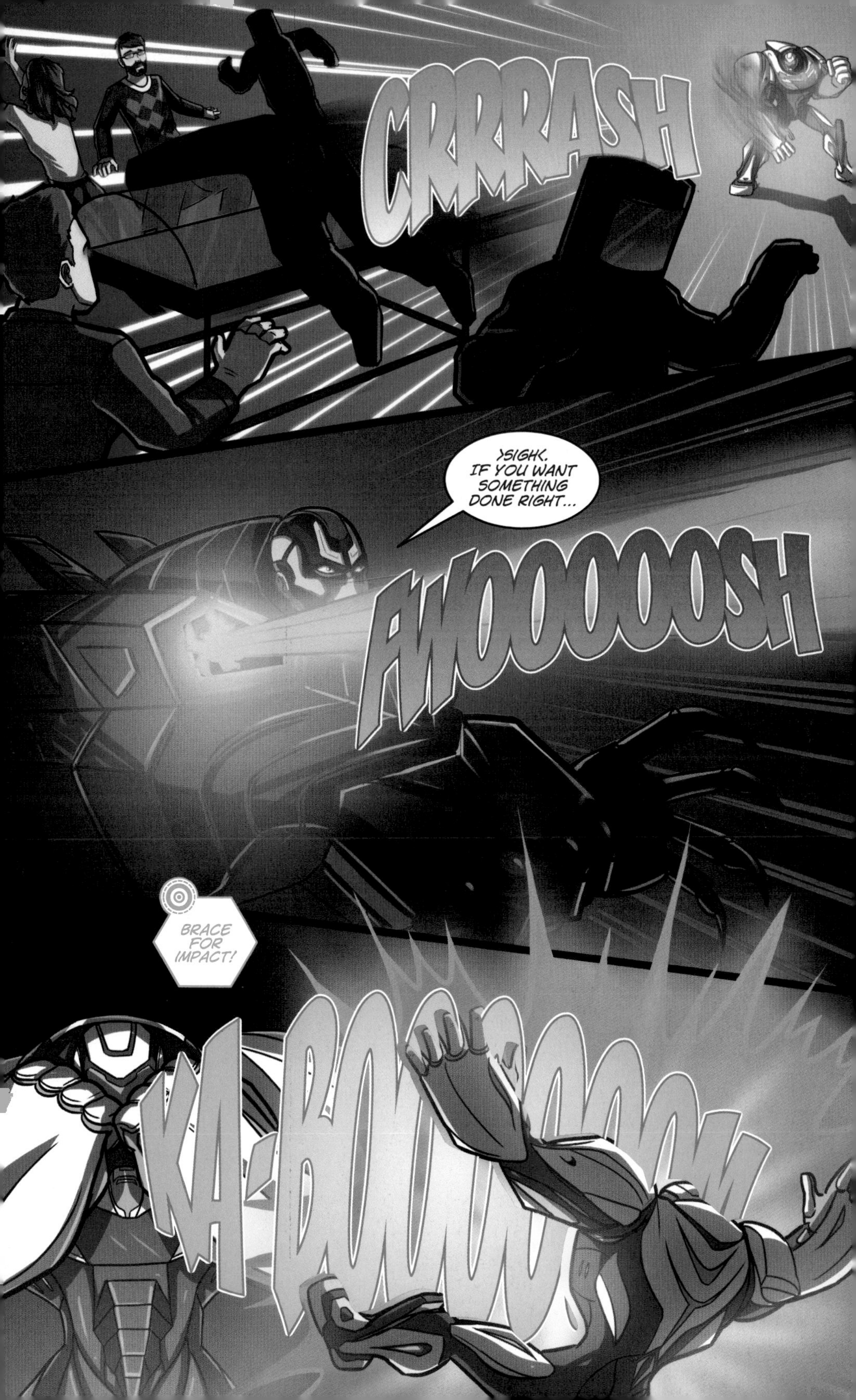
CRRRASH
>SIGH<. IF YOU WANT SOMETHING DONE RIGHT...
FWOOOOOOSH
BRACE FOR IMPACT!
KA-BOOOOOOM

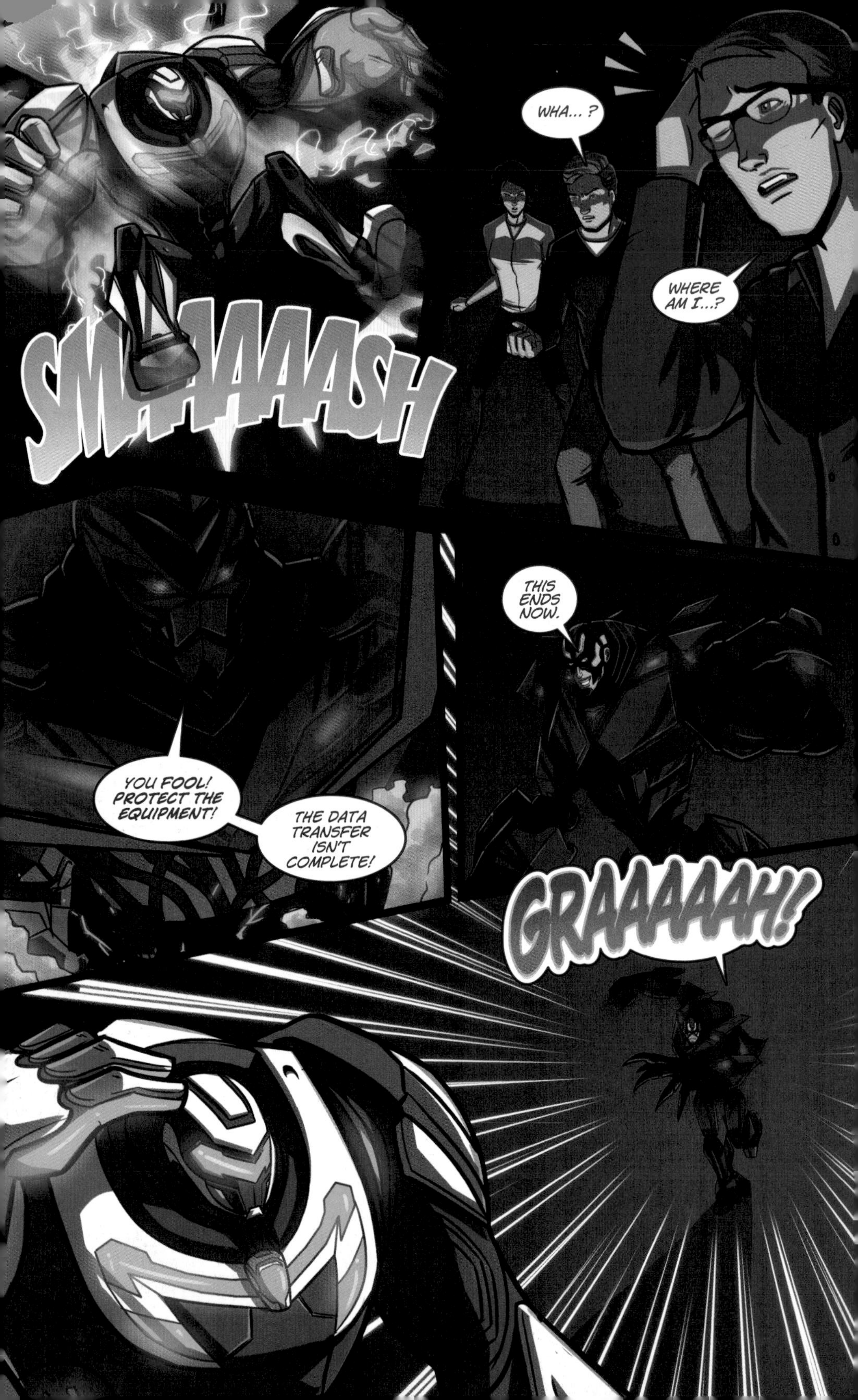
SMAAAAASH
WHA...?
WHERE AM I...?
YOU FOOL! PROTECT THE EQUIPMENT!
THE DATA TRANSFER ISN'T COMPLETE!
THIS ENDS NOW.
GRAAAAAH!!

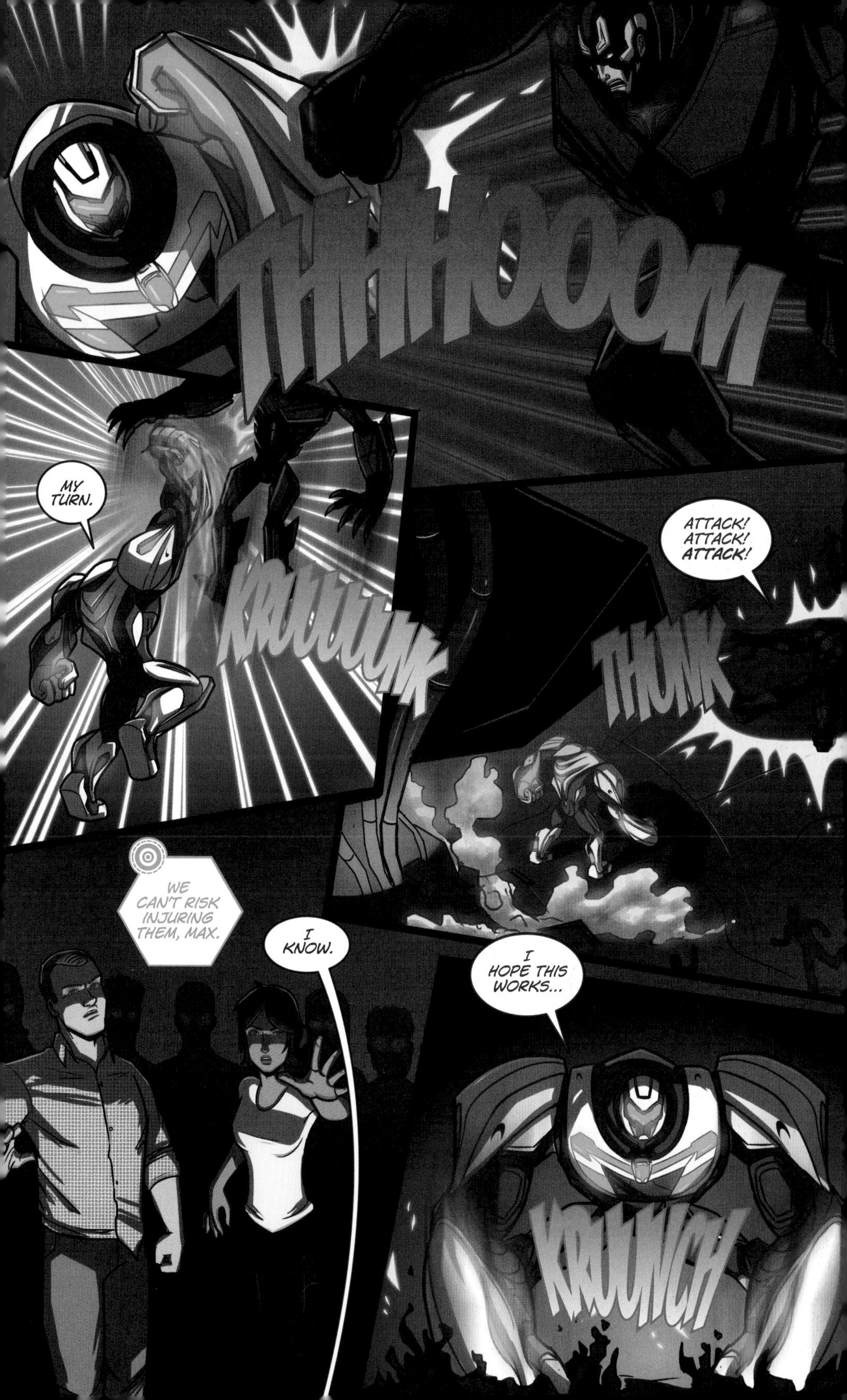
THHOOOM
MY TURN.
KRUUUUNK
ATTACK! ATTACK! ATTACK!
THUNK
WE CAN'T RISK INJURING THEM, MAX.
I KNOW.
I HOPE THIS WORKS...
KRUNCH

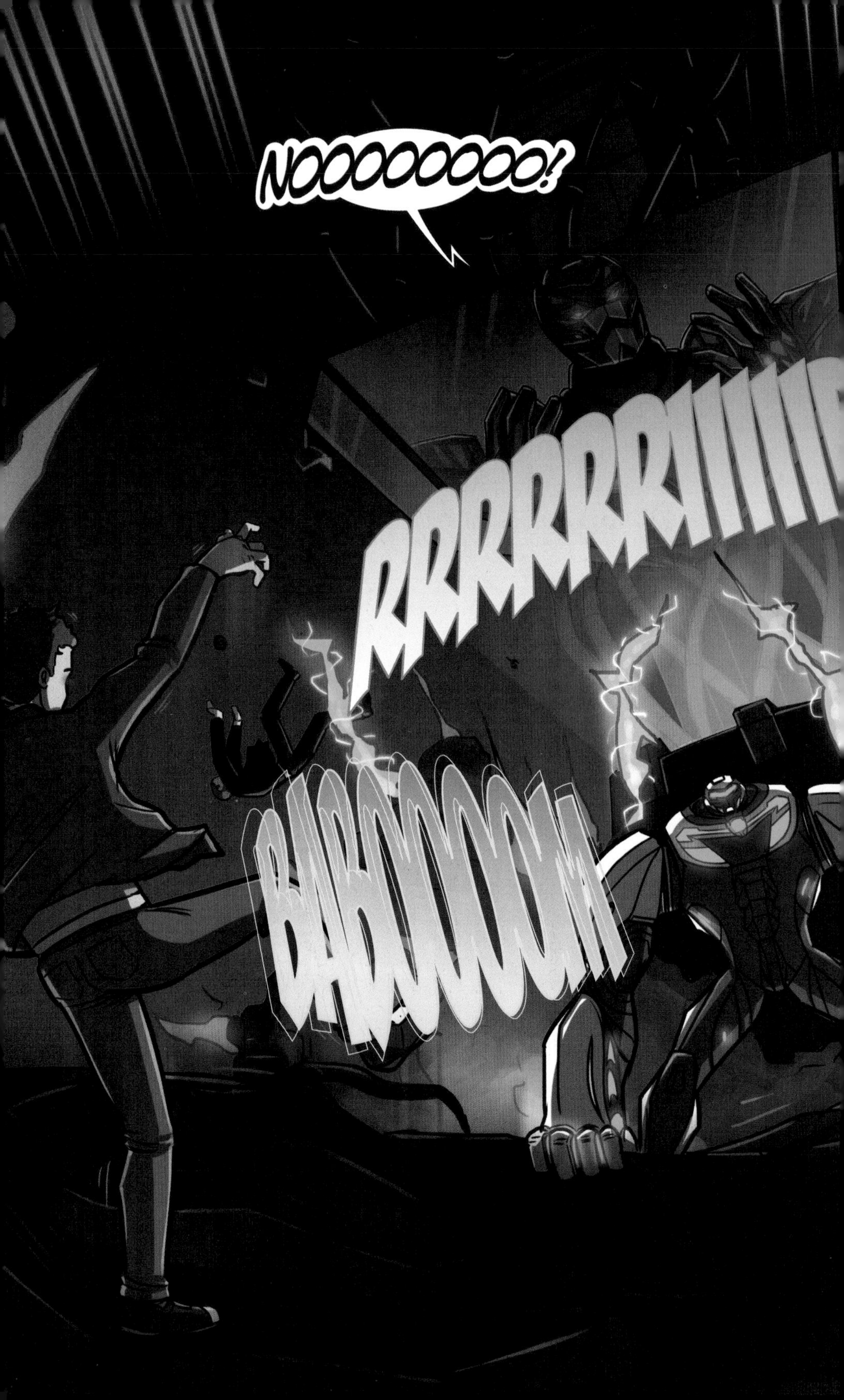
NOOOOOOOO!
RRRRRRIIIIIP
BABOOOOOM

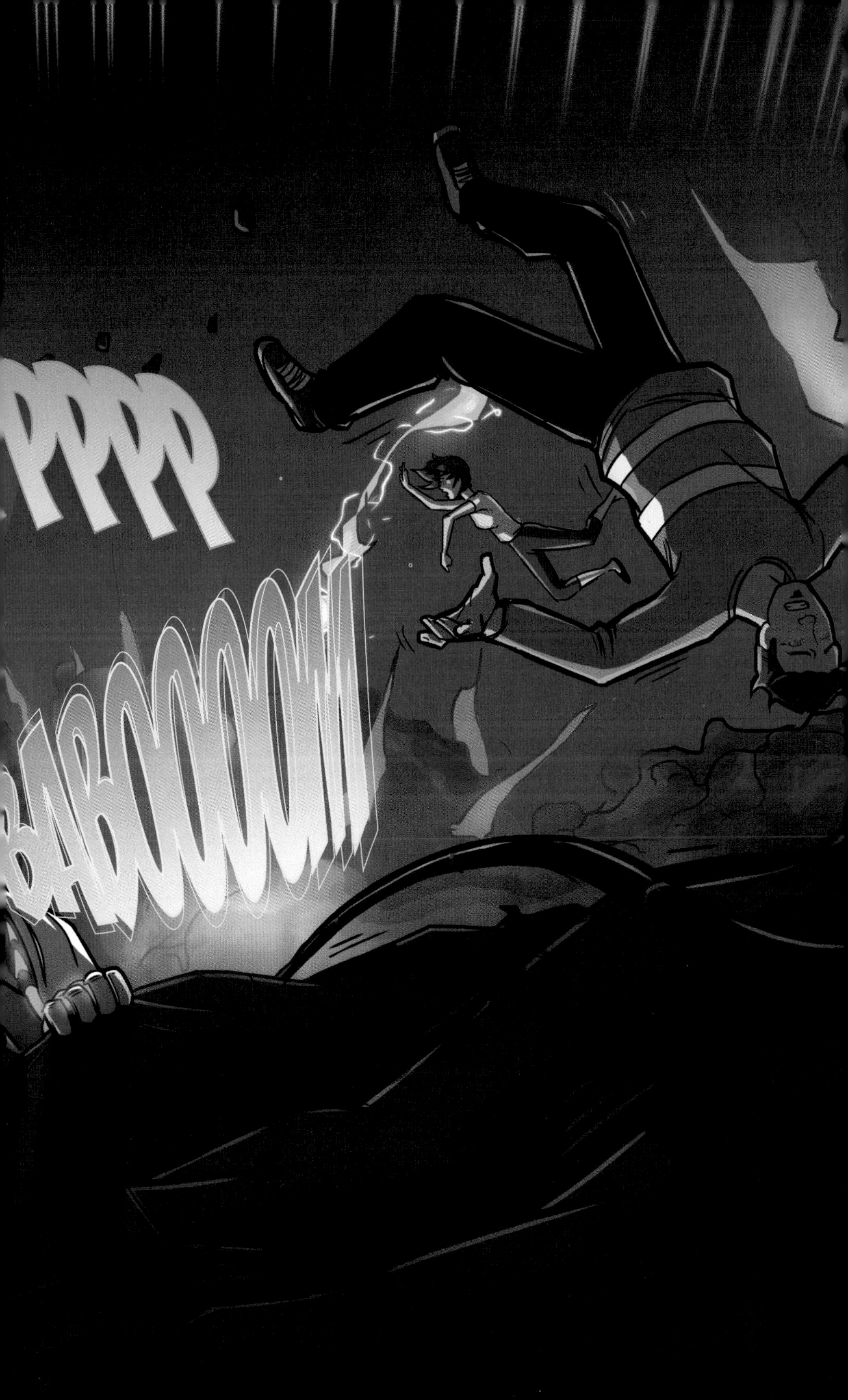
PPPP
BABOOOOM!!

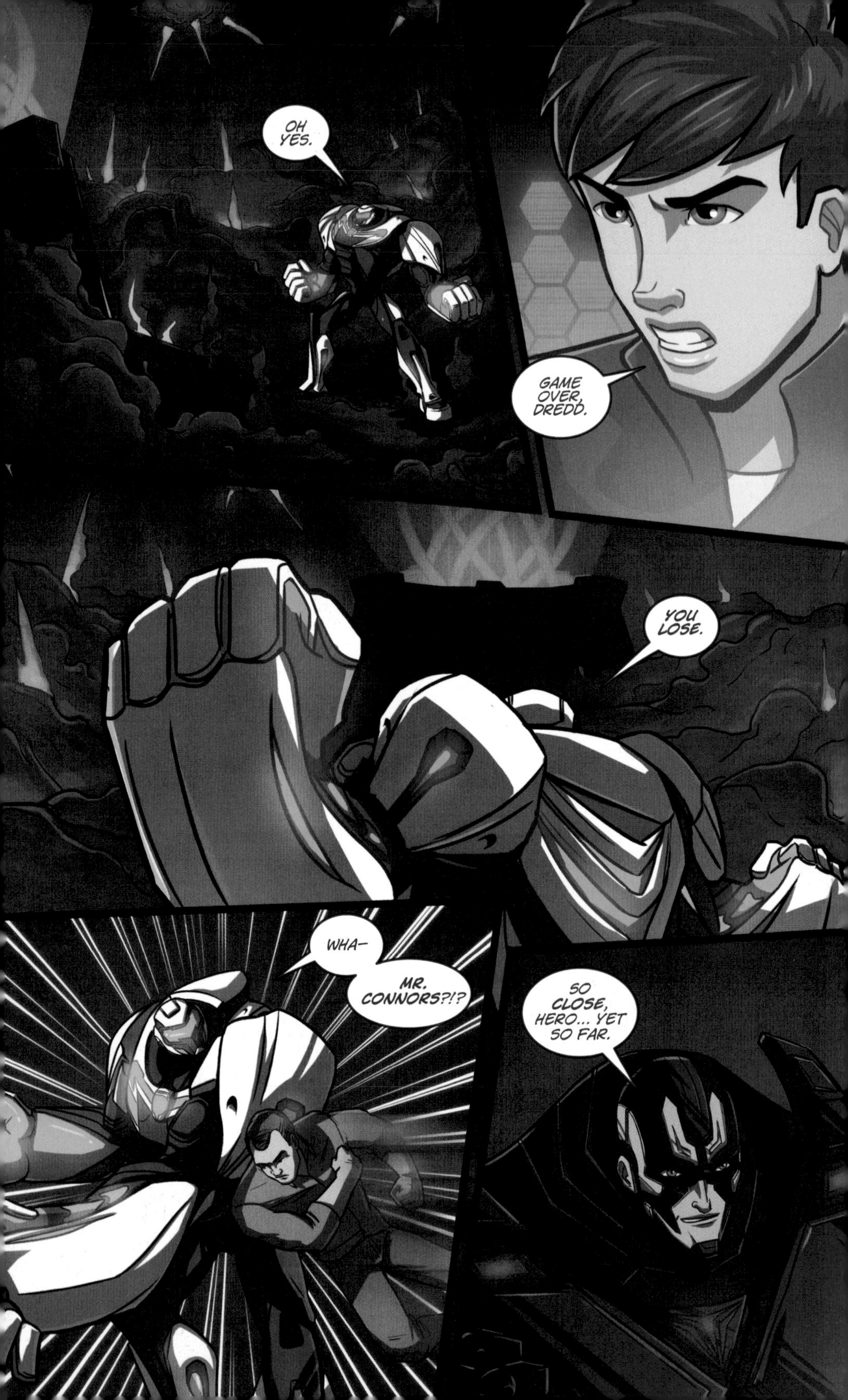
OH YES.
GAME OVER, DREDD.
YOU LOSE.
WHA-
MR. CONNORS?!?
SO CLOSE, HERO... YET SO FAR.

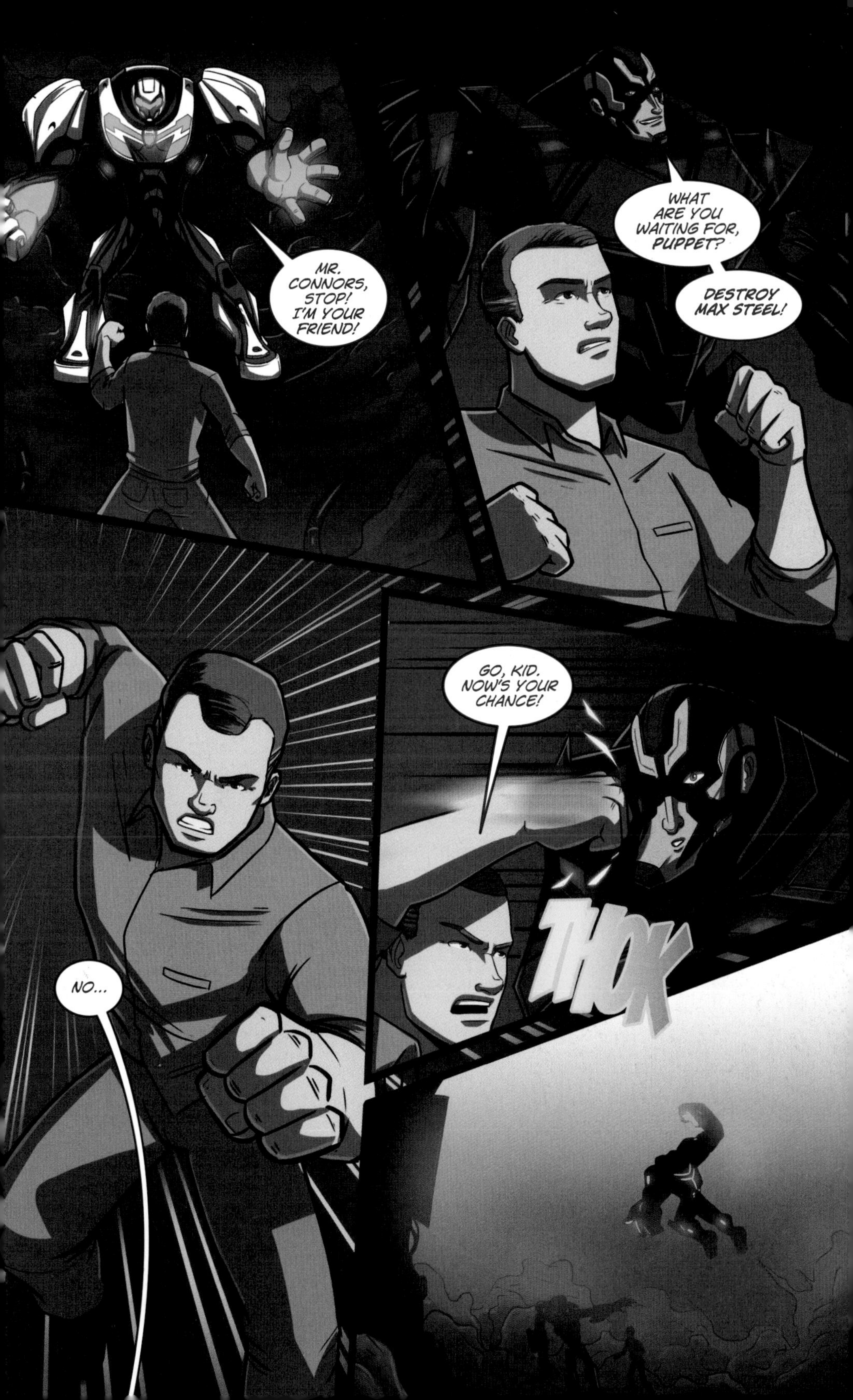
MR. CONNORS, STOP! I'M YOUR FRIEND!
WHAT ARE YOU WAITING FOR, PUPPET?
DESTROY MAX STEEL!
NO...
GO, KID. NOW'S YOUR CHANCE!
THOK

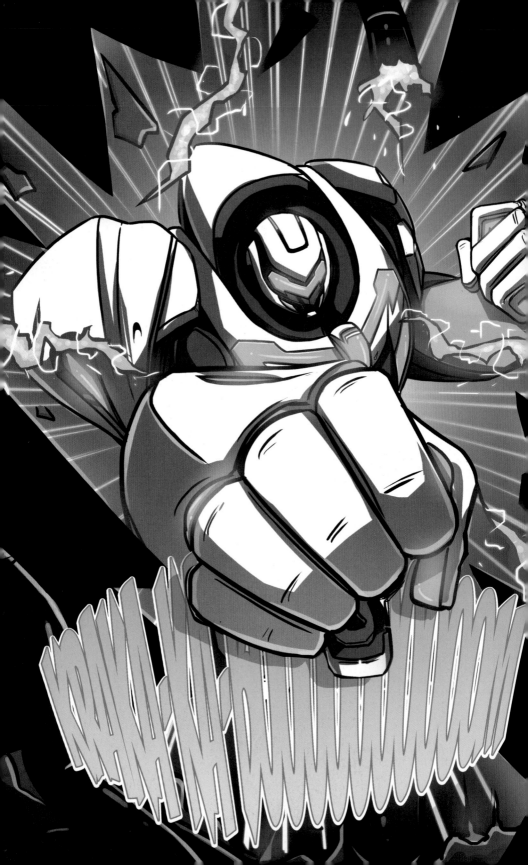

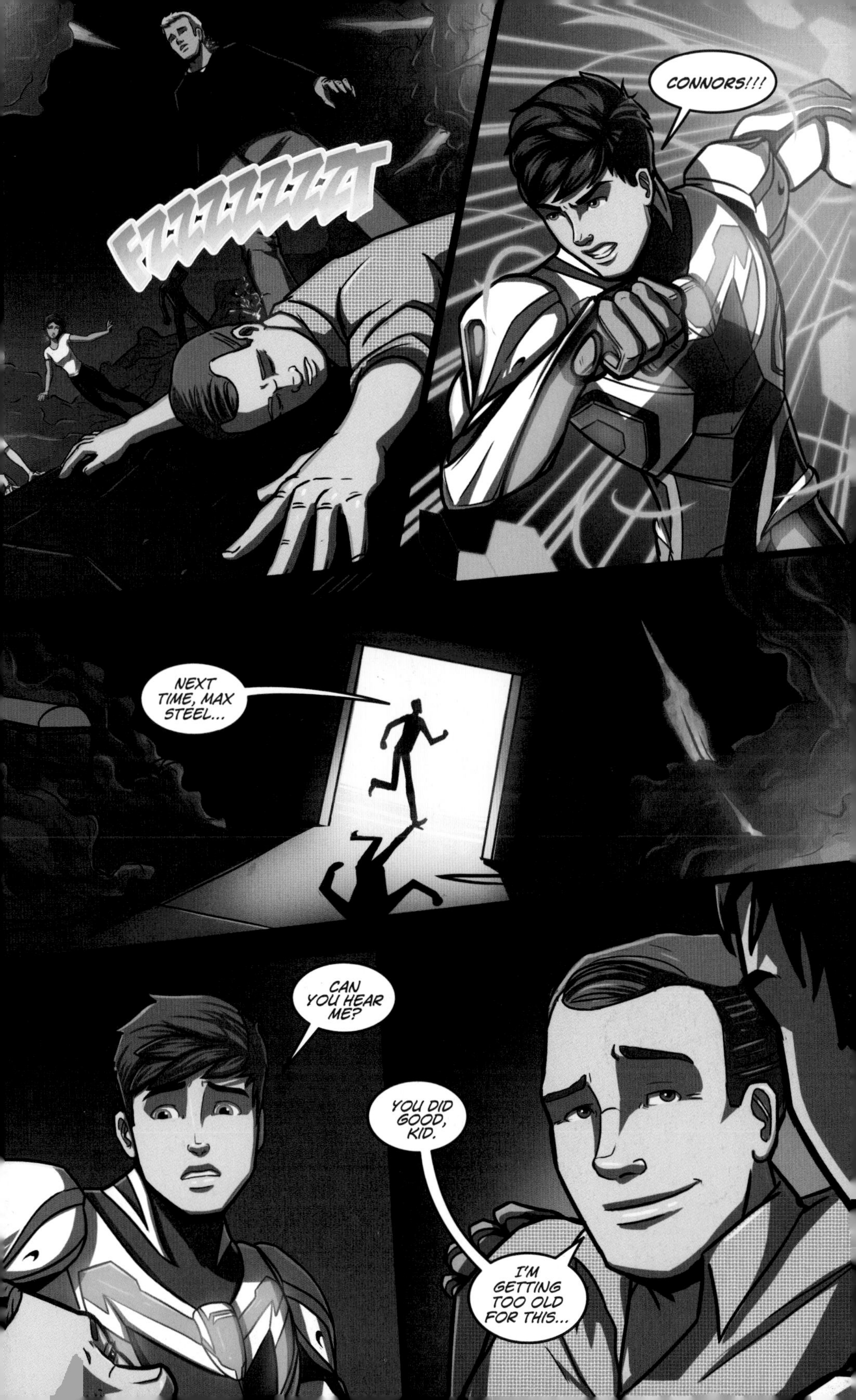
FZZZZZZZZAT
CONNORS!!!
NEXT TIME, MAX STEEL...
CAN YOU HEAR ME?
YOU DID GOOD, KID.
I'M GETTING TOO OLD FOR THIS...

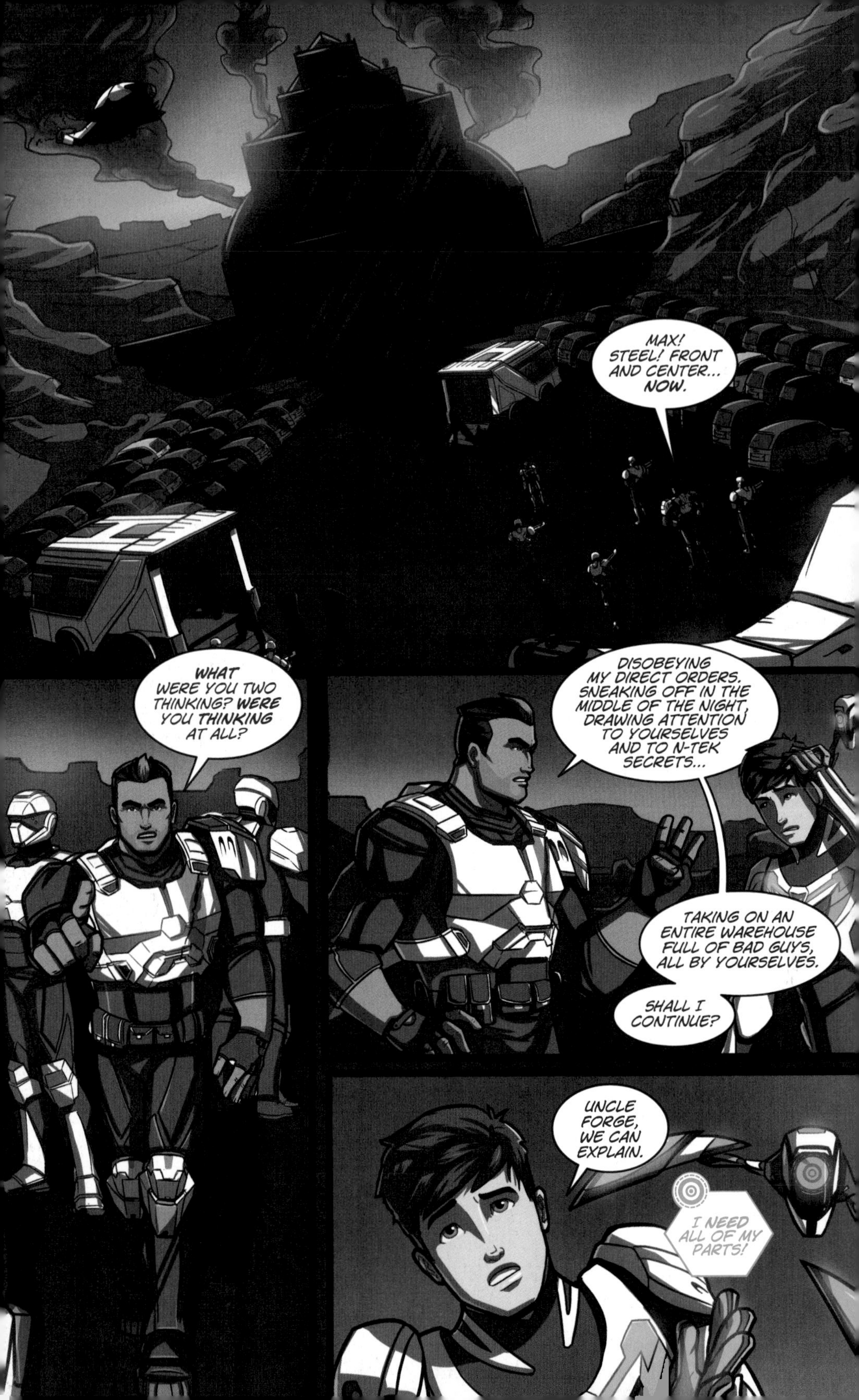
MAX! STEEL! FRONT AND CENTER... NOW.
WHAT WERE YOU TWO THINKING? WERE YOU THINKING AT ALL?
DISOBEYING MY DIRECT ORDERS. SNEAKING OFF IN THE MIDDLE OF THE NIGHT, DRAWING ATTENTION TO YOURSELVES AND TO N-TEK SECRETS...
TAKING ON AN ENTIRE WAREHOUSE FULL OF BAD GUYS, ALL BY YOURSELVES.
SHALL I CONTINUE?
UNCLE FORGE, WE CAN EXPLAIN.
I NEED ALL OF MY PARTS!

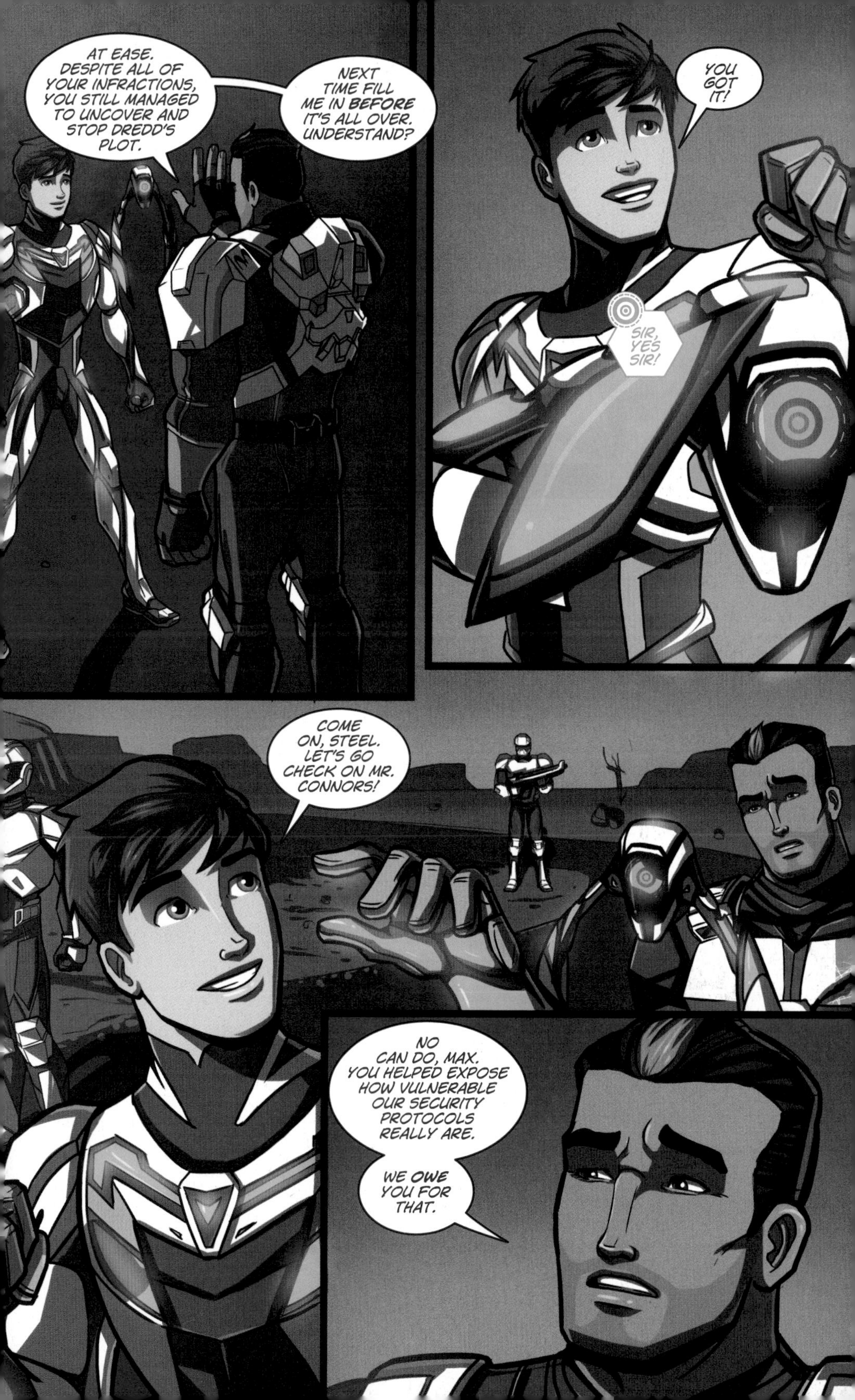
AT EASE. DESPITE ALL OF YOUR INFRACTIONS, YOU STILL MANAGED TO UNCOVER AND STOP DREDD'S PLOT.
NEXT TIME FILL ME IN BEFORE IT'S ALL OVER. UNDERSTAND?
YOU GOT IT!
SIR, YES SIR!
COME ON, STEEL. LET'S GO CHECK ON MR. CONNORS!
NO CAN DO, MAX. YOU HELPED EXPOSE HOW VULNERABLE OUR SECURITY PROTOCOLS REALLY ARE.
WE OWE YOU FOR THAT.

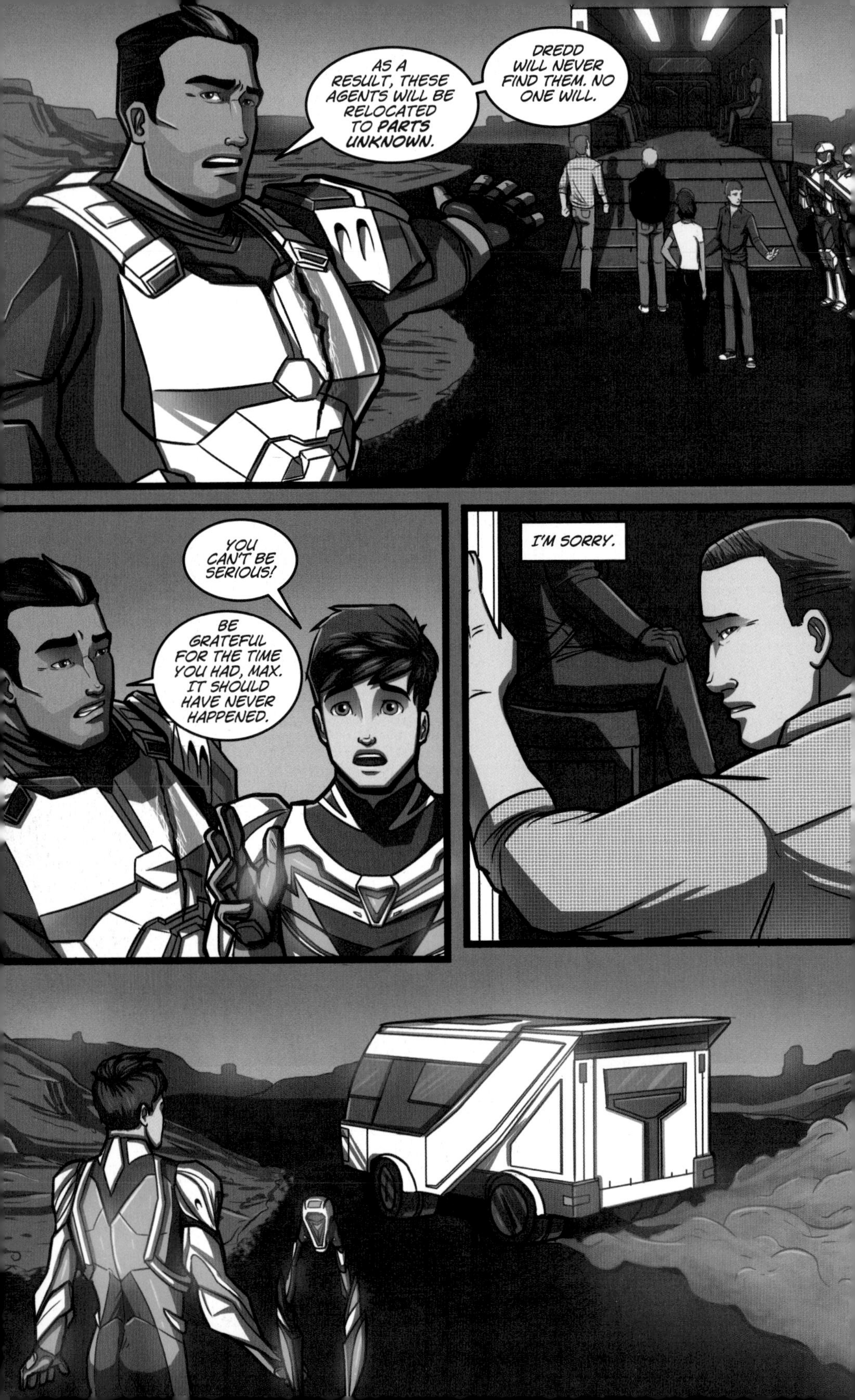
AS A RESULT, THESE AGENTS WILL BE RELOCATED TO PARTS UNKNOWN.
DREDD WILL NEVER FIND THEM. NO ONE WILL.
YOU CAN'T BE SERIOUS!
BE GRATEFUL FOR THE TIME YOU HAD, MAX. IT SHOULD HAVE NEVER HAPPENED.
I'M SORRY.

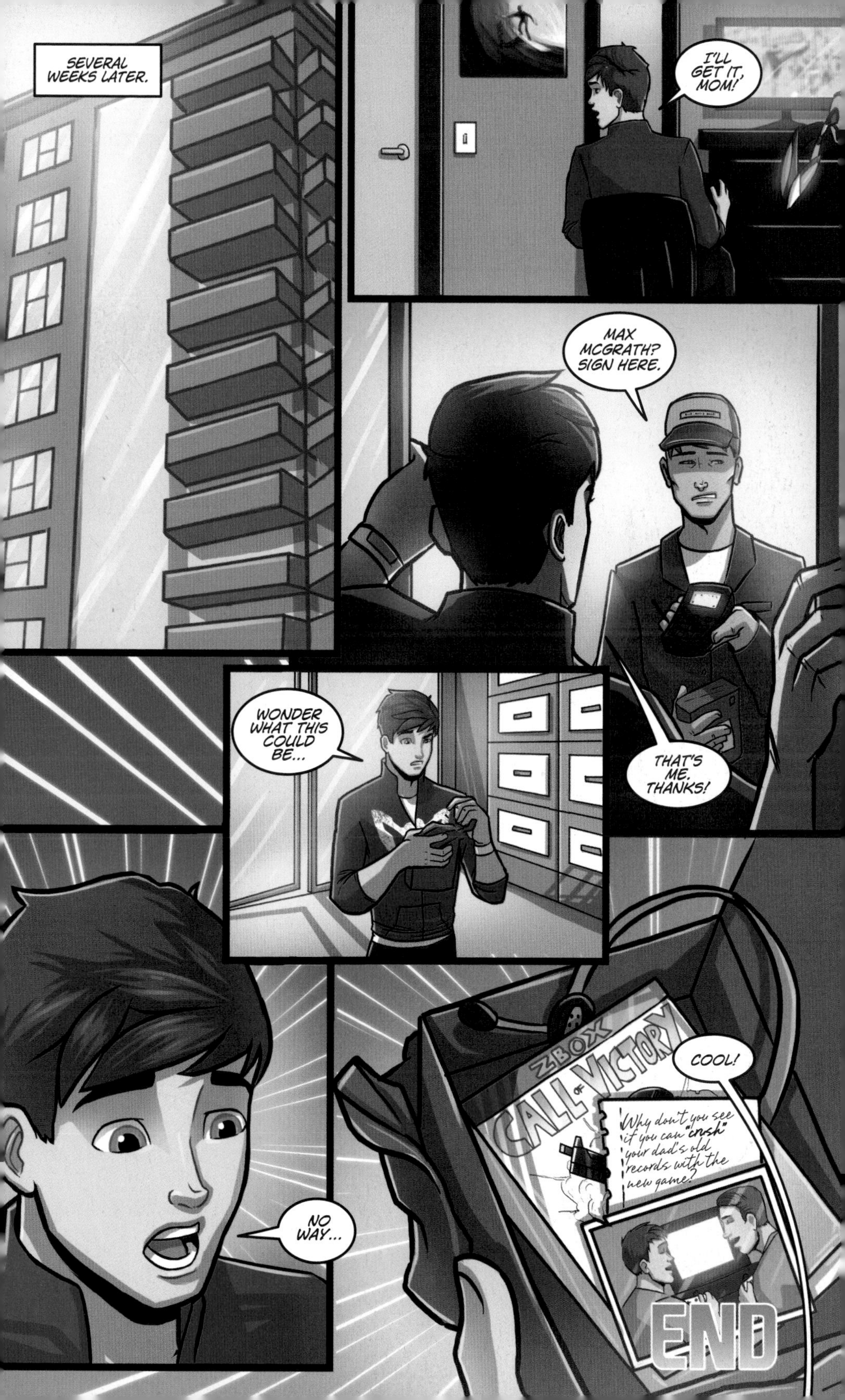
SEVERAL WEEKS LATER.
I'LL GET IT, MOM!
MAX MCGRATH? SIGN HERE.
THAT'S ME. THANKS!
WONDER WHAT THIS COULD BE...
NO WAY...
ZBOX
CALL OF VICTORY
COOL!
Why don't you see if you can "crush" your dad's old records with the new game?
END

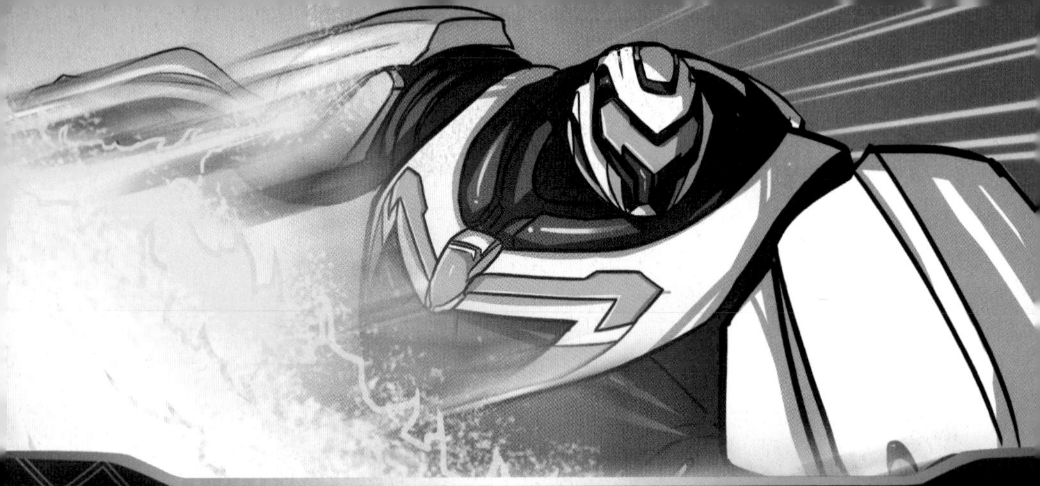

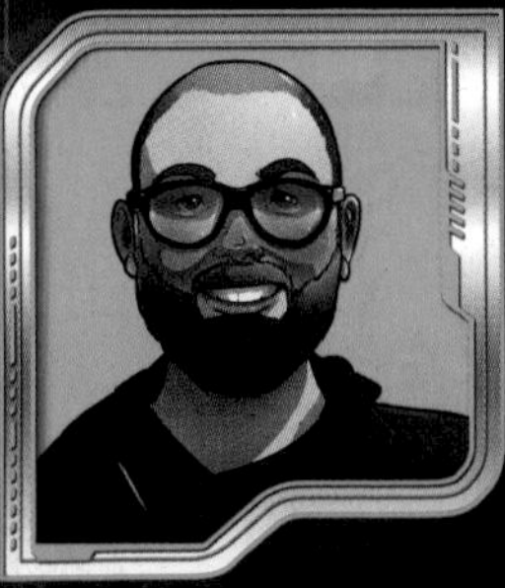

WRITER

BRIAN SMITH is the co-creator/writer behind the *New York Times* best-selling graphic novel *The Stuff of Legend*, and the writer/artist of the all-ages comic *The Intrepid EscapeGoat*. His other writing credits include *Finding Nemo: Losing Dory* (BOOM!), *SpongeBob* (Bongo), *Voltron Force* (VIZ) and *Monsuno* (VIZ).

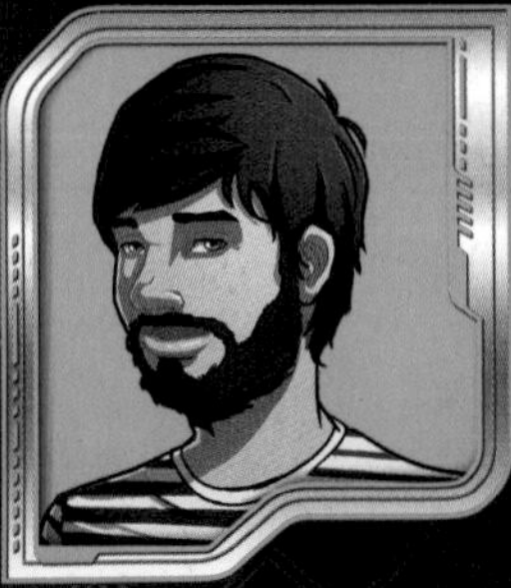

ARTIST

JAN WIJNGAARD is an illustrator living in Manchester, England, and is currently drawing as fast as he can for VIZ to finish up his next project: *Max Steel: Haywire,* which will be on sale spring 2014!

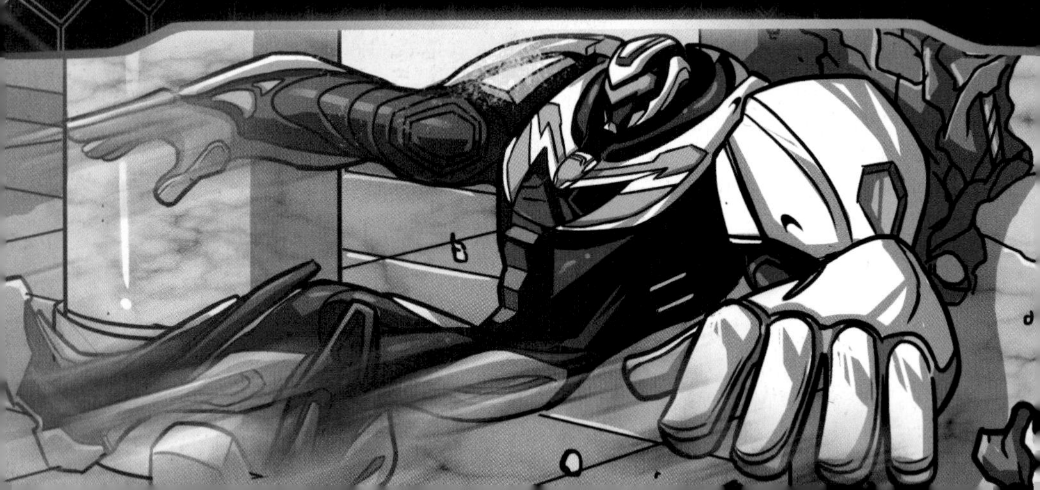

MAX STEEL'S NEXT ADVENTURE IS COMING SOON!

VOLUME 2
◦HERO OVERLOAD◦

All of a sudden Max Steel isn't the only superhero around. Max encounters a trio of superpowered teens with mysterious skills who are in serious need of training. He takes on the task, but can Max get these new heroes up to speed before they have to battle a real threat? One of Max's biggest baddies is waiting in the wings to strike...and Max is going to have to face him with a bunch of newbies!

Story by B. Clay Moore | Art by Alfa Robbi

On Sale in January!

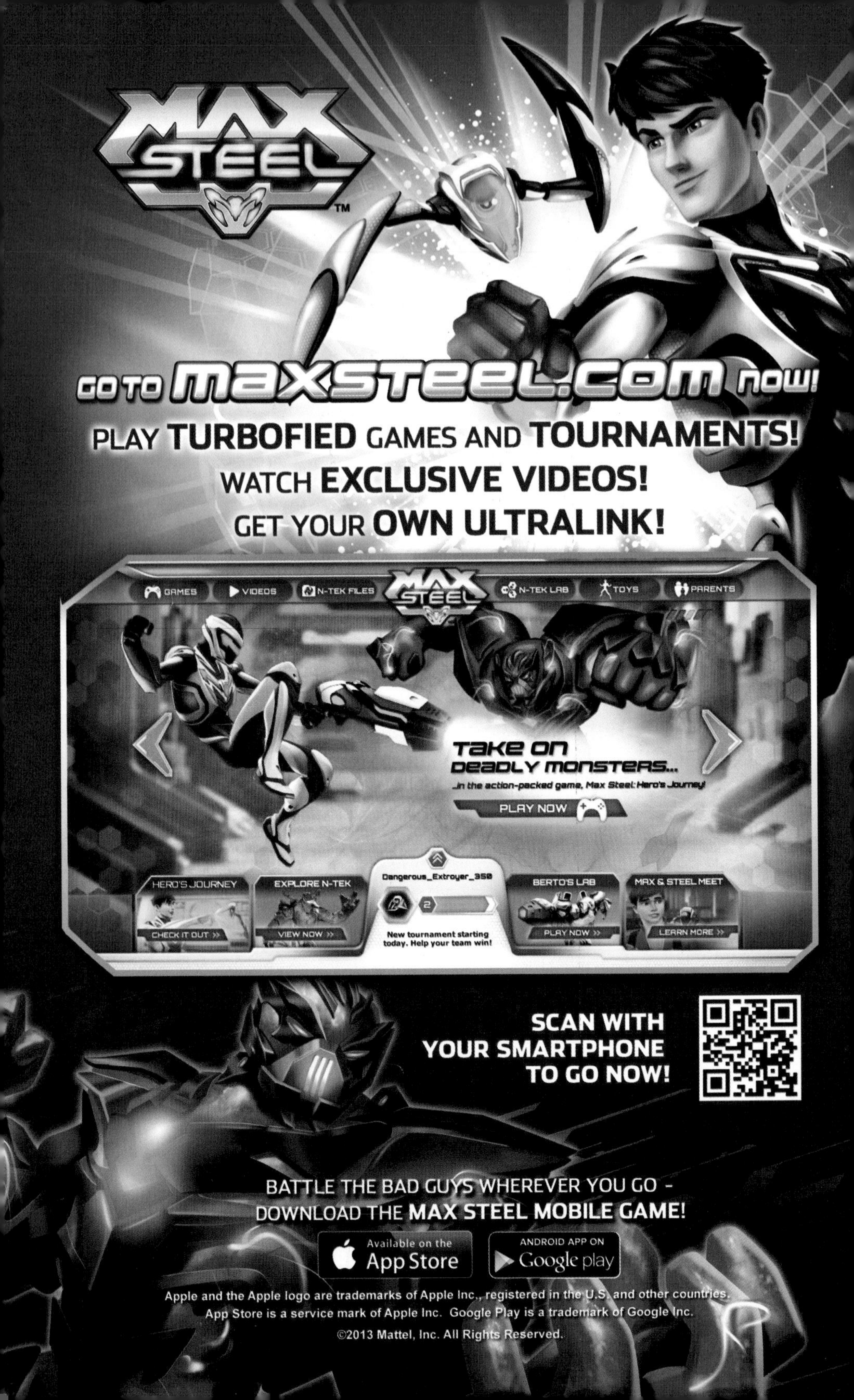
MAX STEEL™
GO TO maxsteel.com NOW!
PLAY TURBOFIED GAMES AND TOURNAMENTS!
WATCH EXCLUSIVE VIDEOS!
GET YOUR OWN ULTRALINK!
GAMES
VIDEOS
N-TEK FILES
MAX STEEL
N-TEK LAB
TOYS
PARENTS
TAKE ON DEADLY MONSTERS...
...in the action-packed game, Max Steel: Hero's Journey!
PLAY NOW
HERO'S JOURNEY
CHECK IT OUT >>
EXPLORE N-TEK
VIEW NOW >>
Dangerous_Extroyer_350
New tournament starting today. Help your team win!
BERTO'S LAB
PLAY NOW >>
MAX & STEEL MEET
LEARN MORE >>
SCAN WITH YOUR SMARTPHONE TO GO NOW!
BATTLE THE BAD GUYS WHEREVER YOU GO -
DOWNLOAD THE MAX STEEL MOBILE GAME!
Available on the App Store
ANDROID APP ON Google play
Apple and the Apple logo are trademarks of Apple Inc., registered in the U.S. and other countries.
App Store is a service mark of Apple Inc. Google Play is a trademark of Google Inc.
©2013 Mattel, Inc. All Rights Reserved.